CRYING IN THE NIGHT

CONFESSIONS OF A SERIAL KILLER

BY

GEOFF LEATHER

This novel is entirely a work of fiction
The names, characters and incidents
portrayed in it are the work of the author's
imagination. Any resemblance to actual persons,
living or dead, events or localities is entirely
coincidental.

A catalogue copy of this book is available
from the British Library
ISBN: 978-1-9163494-8-3

GEOFF LEATHER was born in the north of England and read law in Cardiff and Bristol. He practised law as a Solicitor for many years in Bristol. He has Diplomas in Interior Design and Forensic Science and Profiling.

His interests include painting and drawing, work having been exhibited in Bristol, Bath, Somerset and Ibiza; Building and Project Management including a holiday complex in SW France in the 1990s; Reading and Travel. He is currently working on sixth novel.

Visit Geoff's website at www.geoffleather.com

Also by Geoff Leather

PRISONER 441

A DEADLY PRICE TO PAY

DARKSIDE OF SUNDAY

IDIRA'S AVENGERS [A Free E-BOOK-on his website]

PROLOGUE

Brian Simkins leaned his arms on his desk. Beside him were several red notebooks, some unblemished by handling, others, especially the early ones were faded and rough at the edges from years of contemplation and alteration of the contents. His diaries, as he called them. Today was his last confession. He struggled with his thoughts. How should he sum up his life? Earlier that day he had thought of taking the bus to the coast and wandering down the pier that had been his contemplative refuge over the last few years. The forecast of rain and his fading health had persuaded him to stay indoors.

He picked up his fountain pen and opened the last diary. There would be no more to write, nothing else to add after this one or so he thought. He looked at the sentence he had written last night and spoke it out aloud.

'How does it end?'

He thought he knew exactly how it was going to end. What words are good enough.

**

Behind the appearance of my straight line, things are more complex

"Knowing" – that is impossible. You cannot know someone. Not even he or she knows himself or herself, as inside the person you know, there is someone that you do not know.

No personal achievement will matter once you die. The only things that will live on will be the impact on people that are still alive. one hopes that they will be constructive, not negative.

I am now an impartial but unheard observer being wrapped in a warm blanket in a black void. There are no positive feelings, no bad ones either. All my stress, troubles and nightmares have disappeared. Nothing exists in a beautiful welcoming way.

Chapter 1

Some Years Ago - West Hampstead London

Albert Thornton, former Detective Inspector, lifted the blue and white Police cordon tape and ducked his stocky frame underneath. He straightened and brushed his balding head with the palm of his hand and adjusted his collar. He slowly surveyed the blackened charred remains of Nicholas Penfold's house. Not a bad pile for an MI6 junior operative, he thought to himself. Probably some public-school education from monied parents, the sort his parents couldn't afford. He had tried to disarm himself of the chip of deprivation he had grown up with as he progressed within the force, but it lingered just beneath the surface and rose to the fore this particular morning. Was it going to cloud his judgement again? He took a deep breath.

The November morning was cool; the smell of soddened ash hung in the air. The huge explosion had ripped the Edwardian house to pieces. Gone was the smell of gas mentioned by one neighbour who ran for his life as the fireball erupted inside the house scattering debris onto the pavement and road beyond.

Albert trod carefully through broken roof tiles and skeleton walls that remained. The preliminary report from the local police was of little help save for the conclusion that it was probably caused by a gas leak from a faulty kitchen appliance.

Albert walked into the back garden and turned to face the remains of the rear wall of the house, trying to make sense of the situation. He was now his own boss. It had been a hard transition. The bastards had hung him out to dry, and one particular bastard was going to pay whatever it took. The rules and regulations surrounding his life as a policeman were a distant memory but, still he was trespassing on a current crime scene and had to look the part and tread carefully as in some quarters his name was trouble.

So far, he had gathered from the few friends he still had within the force waiting out their pension but loyal and trusting, was that Penfold had been placed, with the blessing of MI5, into Garth Richards, a heavyweight London law firm, with several very high-profile foreign clients. Albert's information from various sources had told him that they had traced fraudulent financial and shell company transactions that led indirectly to the firm and some of its commercial department partners. Penfold had been instructed to find the internal links with the City's Investment Banks and to confirm the suspected names of European politicians who were aiding and abetting the scheme. MI6 too were trying to find answers. Albert was not interested in the ramifications of financial fraud. It was out of his league, although he suspected that he knew much more than they did about the one man he knew was capable of an outrage like this, but at what point did he want to tread into their murkier world. That question was troubling him as he stood gazing at the death of one man and the devastation of one house.

He could imagine what it must have been like 80 years ago when London itself was alight with fear and grief in WWII as German bombs rained down as he stepped through the debris. Vague memories of what his parents had described flashed through his mind. He was certain now, just like them, this was a targeted attack, not by German bombers on London, but one bastard. Just an unfortunate accident, so the local force had concluded. Albert's thoughts lingered on that one man that he knew so well, and he knew that man was capable of such planning.

Chapter 2

June 1946 The Wirral Cheshire England

Screams could be heard echoing through the empty corridors of the Victorian mansion that was converted and housed the private nursing home called The Hawthorns just a stone's throw from the tidal estuary and the crashing waves of the Irish Sea beyond. The disruption on that quiet Monday night in June many years ago was caused by an anterior arm raised beside the unborn child's head. Inside that child, the feeling spread that all was not well. Of course, the foetus could not hear in the way that one does when one breathes because that had not occurred yet, but early neurons were working remarkably well sending messages through to the foetus's brain. Messages of fear, causing stress and tension.

The baby was wedged against something unforgiving inside. The doctor's scalpel sliced too close for comfort as the baby's head was held out of the way for fear of stabbing the still malleable skull and causing permanent injury. Cold metal then clamped around the head and gradually with a twist here and there, the child slithered into the arms of the mid-wife who then tied and cut the umbilical cord and thereby securing its freedom. The child was then struck by what would have felt like a mighty blow on the back to clear the airwaves and force breath into its lungs. Naturally, at that age, the blow caused uncontrollable howling. It must have seemed a violent unjust world at that point.

That child was named Brian Simkins.

Chapter 3

Present Day - MI6 Headquarters London

Mike Randell stood across the Thames looking towards the MI6 Building at Vauxhall Cross that houses the headquarters of the Secret Intelligence Service, the United Kingdom's foreign intelligence agency located at 85 Albert Embankment. He had been away for some time recovering from his last traumatic few days in Egypt. He took his first few tentative steps across Vauxhall Bridge then quickened his pace. Inside, he followed his usual route through security, taking the staircase, two steps at a time until he reached his Boss, Roger Simmons' floor, and disappeared into the washroom. His tanned face from his time under the Egyptian sun had faded somewhat but not deserted him. His blond hair that he now wore longer than when he started in the service was covering his ears and the collar of his shirt. He took a deep breath, put a hand through his hair, brushed the lapels of his dark grey worsted suit, straightened his navy-blue tie. One last glance into the mirror with his light blue eyes and he was ready for the next assignment.

'Well, Mike. Welcome home. Fully recovered after your time off, I see. That Egyptian conclusion was remarkable. It is a shame we could not go public with it at the time. Would have raised the standing of the service but at least your reputation benefitted. Anyway, I assume that you have had a chance to look at the rather neglected papers I gave about our colleague Penfold. What's your take on the situation?'

'Definitely not an accident, Sir. It was certainly made to look like one. What troubles me, though, is the unnecessary elaboration. Something a professional hit would laugh at, frankly and certainly not one that Garth Richards would be contemplating even if they suspected our infiltration, which I am certain they could not have known.'

'My thoughts exactly,' said Roger Simmons self-satisfied with his original conclusion. He leaned back in his chair. 'What I'm concerned about Michael is that we still have not recovered, even after the department's best efforts, the missing evidence Penfold was collecting from Garth Richards and, to me personally and more importantly our reputation with the boys down the road in MI5 if I have to admit we may have botched the job.'

Mike hesitated when Simmons used "Michael" to address him as he knew that what he just heard was an unsaid note of something much more serious than Roger's demeanour suggested. Mike had grown up through the service with his Boss, Roger Simmons, and felt a deep loyalty towards him. If Roger was even now feeling in any way vulnerable, Mike would delve as deep as he could to protect him.

'On that score, I spoke to our tech boys who worked on the case at the time a few minutes before coming here to see you, Sir. They have confirmed that there was nothing salvageable from either his house or the office. The computer he was using, despite the encryption, was a complete blank. Couldn't trace anything from the hard drive. They told me it was a real professional job.'

'That is what they told me at the time,' said Roger.

'One of the best they have seen, I'm afraid, Sir. As you know, on the ground at Penfold's they concluded, despite, the police preliminary report, that there was trace evidence of an explosive device being used to cause the gas explosion, but the details point to several elements and therefore many possibilities.'

Roger Simmons was quiet for a moment. His mind was elsewhere. He had given no orders concerning Penfold's computer immediately after hearing of the explosion. Someone had. Maybe enquiries into Garth Richards had leaked at the time but he ignored that thought. He nodded his head. Mike watched Simmons's face. He knew not to interrupt. Finally, the silence was broken.

'That is pretty conclusive, Mike. I need to find exactly what happened there. I do not like loose ends, and they have been on my mind too long.

You know as well as I do, that they tend to entangle you, later on.'

'What about the police enquiry?'

'As you know, it was my decision not to interfere. Dear Penfold has no relatives. Left his worldly possessions to his daily help. I let them remain there. That was the official line. With the war on terror escalating around us, we needed to concentrate our energies on prevention on this island of ours.' Simmons was silent, stroking his forehead gently, deep in thought. 'I cannot forget about Penfold, Michael. Now you are back I want you to unravel the problem. Find the culprit and the computer evidence. Tie up the loose ends.'

'I'll do some initial digging and see what follows.'

'Good. Not a word now to anyone here. Understood. Just you and me. I will cover you from this end if someone asks. I suggest you work from home. Here.' Simmons handed Mike a mobile phone. 'All you need is already installed.'

Chapter 4

Present Day Simkin's Apartment Hampstead London

Brian Simkins studied the envelope and looked at the date stamp. It was a Thursday. He unconsciously turned it over several times in his hand unwilling to give in to curiosity as he confronted his fear, the dread of having to accept the inevitable. Peace of mind does not come with finality, not this kind.

His mind was still clear and incisive, he could not contemplate being incarcerated in some morbid lifeless Care Home waiting for the inevitable. He took the letter-opener from his desk and sliced the envelope open. He pulled out the letter and ran his fingers over the creases as it lay on the desk. He lifted the glasses from his chest and read the first sentence, not noticing the attached scribbled note. Only the words *inoperable carcinoma* registered in his consciousness. It was there, that finality. The nagging doubt about his own mortality had dissipated.

Only a few minutes later did he pick up his mobile phone and dial the direct number of his friend and Consultant, Mr Raymond Childs.

'Good morning, Raymond.'

'Hello, Brian. I'm sorry. I would have telephoned first, but you know how it is these days. Everything has to be unequivocal, in writing, leaving us, clinicians, little wriggle room.

'I understand, Raymond. How long?'

'Difficult to say. You're strong, vital and a fighter and with chemotherapy, maybe a year or two if we get the dosage right quickly.'

'No intervention, I don't want weekly stays with a chemical cocktail of your drugs coursing through my body, my hair dropping out, feeling half the week like death and the other half fearful of the next visit.'

'Thought you'd say that. A few months, maybe a little more but not much. It is difficult to speculate. However, Brian, I have seen it before, rare of course, but these tumours are sometimes unpredictable. It could stop growing on its own account, spontaneous remission. Unlikely, I'm afraid to say. Don't rely on it, Brian.'

'I won't. Too much of a realist, but one last question, Raymond. Pain? I have none at the moment.'

'Yes. It will come with increasing severity. I am sorry. I'll get the department to issue a prescription. Make you a bit drowsy as the dosage increases.

'Shank's pony and public transport.'

'Good to hear it. Before you go, you read my note attached?'

'No, I telephoned you straight away, but I will, Raymond.'

'I'm suggesting you take some counselling and before you tell me to bugger off, I really do think you'd benefit. Her name is Barbara Carling and I highly recommend her. In fact, she's waiting to hear from you. Good luck, Brian.'

**

Dr Barbara Carling, Psychotherapist. The smiling face of a woman in her early fifties looked out at him. At least that is what her various academic qualifications suggested. Brian Simkins dialed her number expecting a protective secretary to answer but was surprised to find she answered herself with a reassuring but slightly husky voice that he found alluring but authoritative at the same time.

'Raymond Childs recommended we should have a talk. My name is Brian Simkins.'

'I was expecting you to telephone.'

'So, you know why I am ringing because if I were truthful, Dr Carling, I am not sure myself.'

'That is understandable. Look, my first session is pretty informal with the question; 'Am I right for you and do you need my help and vice versa'.

He booked the first session and relaxed into the comfort of his high-backed office chair, stroking the leather arms as he did so. Now had come the time, at last, to try to come to terms with himself and his life. Brian Simkins felt totally at ease that weekend as he continued with the revision of some aspects of his diaries, preparing himself for his first session with Dr Carling.

Chapter 5

Present Day - Royal Oak Public House London

Back at his apartment, Mike Randell picked up the outside phone line then returned it to its cradle, remembering the mobile phone he had been allocated for this operation. Roger Simmons had made it clear that he was on his own in this enquiry, but it was Mike's duty to Simmons in particular and the service generally. Despite all the chaos of terrorist plot intelligence crossing the desks of MI6 daily after 9/11, to find the killer of one of their own and tie the loose ends after the time that had passed was going to be a tall order. Any new leads were unlikely to appear unless he was prepared to take a risk or two and he knew one man who may be willing to assist. Somebody who would be prepared to walk outside the thin blue line in pursuit of his intuition.

'Detective Inspector Thornton, please?'

'Who's speaking?'

'An old friend. Just tell him that.'

'I'm sorry, DI Thornton no longer works here. Retired a while back.'

Mike was wrong-footed for a moment. Albert Thornton was certainly not of retirement age. Something must have happened. Maybe he walked too far away from that thin blue line? Thinking quickly, Mike decided to announce who he was and asked for Albert's contact details. There was a pause on the line, then several clicks and another longer pause as no doubt someone was checking his credentials.

'Chief Inspector Belton speaking. I'm not sure why you would want to speak to Thornton, and I am not going to ask but these are the last contact details we have, Mr Randell'

'Thank you, Chief Inspector. I am an old friend from years ago, so thanks for the information.'

**

'Albert, long time no see. Mike Randell here. How are you?'

'Michael, not too bad considering, but a pleasure to hear from you. Heard you were in far off lands.'

'Egypt, back now. I need your ear. Can we meet?'

Mike had decided that he was going to let Albert take the lead when it came to his exit from the police force. He was only interested in finding Penfold's killer and the missing computer files, the loose ends that Roger Simmons needed tidying.

At 6 pm on the dot, ex-Detective Inspector Albert Thornton, now dressed in a loud roll-neck sweater in burgundy and tan cargo trousers entered the Royal Oak public house and looked around. His eyes met Mike Randell's. Mike recognized him despite the fact that his head of hair had virtually disappeared and what was left was greying at the edges. He was ruddy in the face and had filled out considerably, but despite that he looked well and affluent.

'Got you your usual? Don't know how you can drink that stuff?'

Albert sat down, putting one hand on Mike's arm and the other around the Guinness sleever and downed a large portion of the pint and wiped his lips and tapped his belly.

'I think I should have been born an Irishman.' He said with a passable accent.

'What's on your mind, Michael, despite the fact you still owe me one.'

Mike remembered their first meeting. He was a student at the London School of Economics and got involved with a group protesting against the Americans stationing nuclear missiles on a British airbase. He was carrying a placard walking towards the American Embassy with fellow students when the march was hijacked by troublemakers. Albert was on the beat and called in with hundreds of other officers, to restore order. Mike's future career ambitions would have been in tatters had not this chance meeting with PC Albert Thornton taken place. Albert had manhandled Mike, not easy when you are a big as Mike, off the street and kicked him up the backside and told him to bugger off.

Mike smiled. 'I know and a time will come. Elephants never forget but now I need another one.'

Mike unfolded an old fading newspaper report of the explosion at Penfold's house and passed it across the table to Albert.

'Ah yes, interesting.'

'Why interesting, Albert?'

'West Hampstead, that was next to my patch and the name Garth Richards, Solicitors, struck a chord at the time. Knew someone there.

'Really. Thought you would be some help. I suspected that that was no terrorist attack.'

'Certainly not. There's a long story involved, Michael. One connected with my retirement?'

'Care to elaborate?'

'Not quite yet, Michael. Let's see how things go, shall we? Tell me what you know, and I will listen. Deal?'

Chapter 6

Present Day Dr Carling's Consulting Rooms London

Session 1

Brian Simkins had not kept his diaries for such a time as this. This one that had fallen unexpectedly into his lap. His writing was never an unconscious need to lighten a burden. It was either a deliberate act of self-justification or a search for self. He did not know which, maybe both.

He started at the beginning and began to read his first red diary. None of the memories had faded, they leapt from the pages, like a ghost. He could feel its hands tighten around his neck. A shiver gripped his body.

He scanned page after page of his actions and thoughts that gushed from the diaries. He had suppressed all the moments of early emotional distress until the pain of most of the incidents had been locked deeply inside. He had tried during this writing process to analyse himself, hoping the exercise would have some therapeutic effect, but each time it failed. Now, his last hope of understanding himself lay unexpectedly with Dr Barbara Carling.

Each revelation was high on antagonism, but he was never anxious. All were meticulously planned, hardly within the label of 'Psychopathy'.

Did he suffer from disinhibited traits? No. He had read and digested as much as he could of each such label. He was not rude, certainly not tactless. He followed the usual social rules, no anti-social behaviour, so being a sociopath had been discounted by him, but what always troubled him was his impaired empathy. He knew that sometimes he exhibited bold and egotistical behaviour, but then who didn't at times.

The reality was that he was an amateur in these matters, Dr Carling was the professional. Maybe she could reach inside and coax something new out of the darkness. Stop him metaphorically, crying in the night. A thread that, when unraveled, would explain who Brian Simkins really is and maybe justify his actions. He had thought carefully about which of the diaries he should present to her first and decided that some of the latest ones would probably provide her with the best opportunity to understand him as they were more detailed and objective in his mind. Some of the early ones would appear as the sessions progressed. After all this was his search for self, not hers.

Brian stood outside the post-war dark brown brick edifice that was Priory Court in the centre of suburban North London, part of the inner-city regeneration following the Nazi bombing in 1940.

Its only saving architectural grace was the curve of the building as it followed the road in front disappearing to his left as if a half moon in the shadow of the night clouds. It was the end of sunny day in early June and the rays glinted off the glass in the metal framed windows. He had walked down Fixstead Road unnoticed and isolated in his own world, eventually he took in the laughter from the open-air bars as he passed, a certain envy in the uncomplicated abandon of the drinkers reminded him of the invincibility of youth.

Now he was about to enter the strange new world of psychoanalysis. Naturally, he had my own preconceived ideas of what it would be like, how he would feel, what he would say. He had done this all before, searching inside his head, trying to extract an answer that would fit all the situations, but he had failed to allay an unease within himself. All those contemplative ambles along the pier, sitting watching the sea as it moved according to the moon and wind, had ultimately failed to help him understand. This was now his last chance.

He climbed the flights of stairs, trying and failing to take two at a time with the assistance of the handrail. At Dr Carling's floor, he stood until his breathing eased. After the walk, maybe he had done too much. He entered the reception.

'I have an appointment.'

'Yes, you're expected, Mr Simkins. Please follow me.'

The door opened into an office that was more akin to any middle-class sitting room at home. Pastel shades of green contrasting on adjoining walls. Forgettable reproduction scenes of tranquility methodically positioned so as not to distract a person's concentration. Comfortable and relaxing.

'Where's the flat screen TV?' was his only comment as Dr Barbara Carling shook his hand. She smiled as she beckoned him to sit on the small settee that sat beyond a large coffee table separating them. Each had their own space for thought. He opened his briefcase and handed her the letter from Raymond Childs. As she read it, he studied her face. Auburn hair fell both sides, cut to the shoulders, light flecks of unhidden grey glistened in the sunlight. A pretty face, calm and inviting. He felt at home with this woman.

'Mr Simkins.' I stopped her.

'Please call me, Brian. May I call you Barbara?

'Of course, formality can inhibit and stifle disclosure.'

'Brian, I'm sorry. Are you undergoing chemo?'

'No. I've said no intervention. I have been told, a few months, so the pressure is on both of us.'

'I see. So, what are you expecting from me? I am not sure that I am the right person to be dealing with end of life…'

'That's not why I'm here. I am here because I need to talk to someone who can understand and explain to me, who and what I am.'

'I see and what do I need to understand?' She had a confused look on her face. He knew that what was now to confront her was something entirely unexpected and different.

'It's here in my briefcase.' He took out a red diary and put it on the sofa beside him but held it tightly in his hand for the moment.

'You said this first meeting was a "Am I right for you and vice versa." Correct?'

'Yes, that's what I said.'

'Well, I've already decided that you are the right person for me to talk to, if you will accept me as your patient.'

'That sounds very formal, Brian. Do I get to be part of the decision?'

'Well, am I your patient?' He watched her. A smile came to her eyes as she nodded.

'Good, but I need to be clear on exactly what I can tell you without those divulgences going any further.' He held up the diary momentarily. Dr Carling looked unsettled as she stared at him. She rose and walked to her desk, picked up a large book and leafed through the index; then she opened a page, walked back to her chair, and placed it on the table.

'Unless you are a terrorist and about to reveal details of an operation you are involved in.' She laughed as she settled down again. 'Then you are safe with me.'

'So, you are not required by law to breach our confidences in any other circumstances?'

'Well, that's not quite right but essentially that's good enough.'

'Not wishing to be pedantic, but that's not quite so reassuring or enough. What comes into '*that's not quite right?*' You need to be more specific, please.'

She looked at him wondering where this conversation was going to end up. Her eyes wandered across the red book sitting next to him on the sofa. She was silent, fingering the reference book, searching unseeing the moral dilemmas, the ethical problems each page contained and then looked at him with an unsaid comment, '*Life expectancy a few months.*' Finally, she took a breath.

'No-one in my profession is required by law, save as I've already said, to breach your confidences unless you agree in writing, to inform the police that you have committed a crime.'

'That's what I wanted to hear,' said Brian. Then she continued talking.

He took in phrases like 'disclosure is essential to protect third parties', 'risk of death', 'prevent a crime being committed'. He was here to tell her, this stranger, about him for the first time in his life and was not afraid of leaving anything unsaid.

'Sorry, what did you say?' She looked at him as if he I had fallen into a deep trance. He had but it was not deep.

'I said 'are you happy now?'.'

'Yes, quite satisfied. Sorry, but thank you.'

'Good. Shall we begin. Tell me why you needed to see me.'

'I didn't need to see you. I wanted to see you.' Brian said rather too sharply. 'Sorry, I'm a little up tight.'

'Most people are at first. It's fine.' She replied professionally and he noticed with some sympathy close to the surface. 'Where do you want to begin?'

'Here.' He handed her the first diary from the settee. 'The rest will follow as our sessions progress.

'This is an unusual approach.'

'Is it?'

'Well, normally, Brian, I would start with a few questions and try to guide you towards revelations about your experiences that you think may have shaped your life but this way it might get a bit confusing, not just for me but also for you. Further, whilst these sessions are not formal, they would normally follow a recognized pattern; a pattern that I've developed over many years of experience and seems to work.'

'I'm prepared for that, I have been confused about me for many years, so skipping from here to there would not come as any surprise, but, I suppose, it may involve you in more preparation.' There was an apologetic tone in his voice.

'Perhaps when you read this, you'll see that I have tried to anticipate those questions. I knew this day would come but never had any preconceptions about how and where; obviously, I had thought through a few scenarios but this meeting with you was not one of them, hence the unusual presentation in writing. If I were to be honest with you and, of course, I will try to be throughout our sessions, I had originally decided to give my notebooks, diaries, papers, those that I will bring to each session, to my solicitor only to be opened after my death. Probably the coward's way out, but at least I could rest knowing that I had come clean, so to speak.'

'O.K. Let us see what we have,' she said fingering the first page.

Chapter 7

Pre Natal Amnesia

Session 1 continued

Brian Simkins sat back and watched as Dr Carling started leafing through his first diary.

Sigmund Freud coined the term "childhood amnesia" to describe this loss of memory from the infant years up the age of three or thereabouts. Scientists tell us that when children are young the hippocampus, a part of the brain crucial to memory, is still undergoing neurogenesis, that is new neurons are constantly being produced. This has the effect of clearing out old memories to prepare the way for new learning.

Dr Carling looked up after reading the first few sentences.

'You have been reading a lot.' This was her only comment as her eyes travelled back to my diary.

**

The question is: which memories linger, and which don't? Those that provide comfort, nurture and relaxation seemed the obvious candidates, not those of pain and trauma which the mind tries to suppress, I imagine. The clearing out is vital for a growing child, but not so important for a young adult, but for me unfortunately it did not happen that way. I am convinced that my hippocampus was never cleared out of any of its memories, it just continued to produce new neurons so that unlike you who are reading this I have memories of pre-natal experiences.

Dr Carling read on as I relaxed into the settee opposite her.

The gurgling and rushing of water and food that would soon provide the sustenance that I needed to grow. Sometimes what my mother ingested did not suit me and I told her so, not in words but actions. I moved inside making life uncomfortable for her. Giving her headaches, occasional sickness and nausea. I wasn't trying to cause her to resent my presence or make carrying me unbearable, I just reacted, and it worked. Anything I did not like was discarded. Years later she told me that she had given up alcohol and fatty foods. Those forbidden foods, I sorry to say were later welcomed by me.

I am not sure exactly when I swung my arm before birth that came to rest near my head, but I remember that I reacted violently to some bodily movement that was both sudden and unexpected. Yet most of my time growing was relaxed as blood nutrients were passed to me in the gentle calm atmosphere of the womb.

Now I have asked myself what effect the retention of all those early neurons had on me because it is not until we gain the ability to lay down long-term memories reliably that we can begin to build a strong self-identity. I know I am different because the sophisticated neural architecture needed was formed before my birth with the experiences intact. I was therefore able to obtain and hold onto more complex forms of memory.

These very early birth memories are real. I can feel them at this moment as I write about them. They are imbedded in my mind because they have richer detail associated with them and richer detail is vital to memory triggers.

**

'Interesting, Brian, because as you will no doubt have read a foetus is known to have pain receptors throughout the body by eight weeks of gestation and by twenty weeks gestational age, pain can be felt.'

'I can tell you it was as painful for me then as it would be if I were an adult. The situation was further exacerbated by my stress response to needling of my foetal skin during the birth itself,' I interrupted. 'So, did this traumatic entry into the world influence who I am?' I questioned.

'Brian, this is an interesting piece of, how shall I put it, guess work. Not that's not the right word, conjecture. I did study the detail of Freud's theory but a long time ago. I will give it some thought. Maybe we will have to come back to this later.'

'Of course.'

Chapter 8

Present Day - The Royal Oak Public House London

The public bar was filling up with the end of another working day as Albert and Mike looked around.

'Remember the days of smoke filling the air, Michael?'

'Long gone now, seems unthinkable that we were subjected to those toxic fumes.'

'Agreed. Anyway, where were we?'

'I did some digging after you mentioned that you knew someone in Garth Richards. I remember you were quite a cricketer in your day so when I did a search of the partner's names, Brian Simkins sprang into view. You play cricket with him, by any chance?'

'Didn't take you long, Michael. Yes, you're right. We were great mates, once upon a time. Used to sink a few pints after a match. Swopping stories from both sides of the fence, so to speak. Philosophizing about this and that.'

Albert paused and picked up his Guinness, then without taking a sip, put it down again firmly on the table and looked at Mike.

'I blame him for my dismissal from the force,' he said with emphasis.

‘What! Why? What did he do?’

‘I started to get a bad feeling about him as we were talking after one match. I cannot remember the details as we were quite merry, talking about justice, legality, fairness, that sort of thing. I started to wonder when he became animated about injustice and seemed to be blaming me, or us in the force, for being too soft and letting domestic violence go unpunished. I tried to reason with him, giving all the rationale as to why it was a particularly difficult area of the law to enforce, but he was having nothing of it. Kept banging on about needing ‘police type’ vigilantes.

‘Is that when your friendship ended, that night?’

‘No, just let’s say I cooled a bit, but it set me thinking more about Brian Simkins. Unfortunately, Michael, I became obsessed. I would not be sitting here now if I’d taken my superior’s advice to lay off, but I couldn’t stop myself. I knew something was not right. You know that gut feeling. It persisted, eating away at me. I just could not stake it off.’

Mike was silent, sipping his beer, thinking. He had an uneasy feeling that he was stepping into a place he would rather not be. He glanced at Albert. The expression on his face was still there, the piercing eyes of a man that wanted revenge. It wasn’t an emotional element that would subside with time that he had heard in Albert’s voice when he blamed Simkins for his dismissal. It was frighteningly raw and reprehensible.

'So, what came next, Albert?' said Mike hoping he had misread the situation and that Albert would return to the man he knew and respected.

'Next time, Mike. 'I have to go,' he said fingering the dial of his watch.

Whilst Albert trusted Mike Randell implicitly, he was not about to reveal all he had discovered about Brian Simkins until he judged the time was ripe. His suspicions about Brian Simkins' alter ego needed to be thoroughly confirmed and until then, he would wait. He would need Mike to be pulled in further and then he could use Mike's superior licensed authority to confirm matters beyond his own network. Some day, soon, Mike would insist on knowing how he had obtained and was obtaining such detailed information. That avenue was firmly off limits for the moment. Albert would only feed Mike, matters relevant to the Penfold case. The other revelations of earlier events would just confirm that they were dealing with a dangerous man, in Albert's eyes.

Chapter 9

The Violent Lover

Session 2

I remembered a call as if were yesterday, even though the events took place some many years ago. My comfort zone was to be breached within a few hours, although I did not know it at the time.

'I think you need to meet me at 3 Burlington Avenue,' said my Letting Agent.

'I'll be there after work, will six be okay?'

Burlington Avenue was a tree lined road with Victorian terraced houses on each side. Number 3 had a small front garden with trimmed privet hedge, built on two floors and an unused basement. If I were honest the property needed a make-over, new kitchen and bathroom and the conversion of the basement, but for the moment and with the level of rent, it suited the tenant who was happy with the situation.

My agent pressed the doorbell. Eventually the bolt slid open, and the key turned in the lock. A slight young woman opened the door. I was horrified by her appearance. Sally Trimble had bruising around both eyes, one of which as almost closed, her lips were cut, and she had appeared to have been crying for a long time. A small child, maybe three or four years old, held on to her mother's short dress, hiding most of her little face and the yellow and blue blotches of bruising on her mother's legs.

The house smelled clean and looked orderly, if a little sparely furnished. We were invited into rear room adjoining the kitchen. The little girl had climbed onto her mother's lap and clung tightly to her chest. She eyed the two of us suspiciously with little movements of her head towards us as we sipped tea. Sally Trimble told us about the abuse she had suffered at the hands of her boyfriend, Graham Parsons.

Sally Trimble had met him about a year ago and they had started a relationship, and only later she discovered that he was married. She tried to stop seeing him. That was when that he started to become threatening. She never intended to tell his wife, but he would not listen. Once the violent line had been crossed, it became a regular factor in his visits and their relationship. The final straw was a threat against Abbie. She lowered her voice to a whisper and leant towards us. 'You dare say anything, he said, then pointed at Abbie. You'll never see her again.'

From that point, with my anger heightening hidden under my veil of concern, I realized that I had no choice.

'I had to give in to his every demand for my safety, but then he crossed the line again.'

She lifted Abbie little blue skirt. There for both of us to see were bruises on both legs. She started to cry again. She was clearly at her wits end.

Parsons was now in my mind, dangerously out of control.

'We need to rehouse you as quickly as possible,' said my Letting Agent.

'There's Ravensdale. They're moving out this weekend. Sorry, didn't tell you, Brian.' He turned to Sally Trimble. 'It's further away. but I think you'd be safe on the other side of the river.'

For the first time that evening she smiled and started to relax.

'Is that possible?'

'Yes, we'll have you away from here as soon as we can. Won't we, Brian?'

'Of course,' I said.

'Has this fellow, Parsons got a key?'

'No. He's never lets himself in. I certainly never gave him one.'

'Do you know where he works, his home address, where I can find him?'

Sally Trimble looked worried at the thought.

'I'm thinking about the move without him finding you again,' I said reassuringly.

'He's on holiday. Gone abroad somewhere with his family. Just told me that I wouldn't see him for a couple of weeks. That's why I rang.'

'Ideal time to move, then'

'We'll sort it. Just leave it to us,' my Letting Agent to Sally and Abbie, smiling.

I was miles away lost in thought about Parsons and what sort of creature could go on holiday and forget about his violence and intimidation of his innocent victims, so I just nodded.

Two days later and several hundred pounds lighter, we had moved Sally Trimble and Abbie south of the river. Safe for the moment. Several days later, I was in the office when I received a call from my agent.

'What about no.3?'

'Perhaps it's time to refurbish. What do you think?'

'Incorporate the basement at the same time is my suggestion? I've told you that before, reap the benefits now. It's a good location and deserves your indulgence.'

'You mean my cash, don't you? Easier said than done.'

'Dig out the back, put some steps down and double doors. They've done it up the road. Looks good. Well, let me know when you've finished.'

'Don't get ahead of yourself. Let me look at the numbers.'

The next day after Ron, the builder, and I had discussed the proposals. I walked around and wandered again through the unlocked door under the stairs and down the stone steps to the basement. The air smelled dry but stale. It was warm. The old Victorian cupboard along one wall was still intact. I pulled open one of the doors and peered inside. There was no mildew or decay. I turned and looked at the small window at ceiling height and imagined double doors leading up into the rear garden that Ron had, in his usual confident way, had said no problem once we've cleared the rear access.

As I was retracing my steps, I heard the front door open and the boards above my head creak. Had I left the front door open by mistake? No-one else had a key. I waited in silence. The only word I heard was "Sally" as the footsteps took to the stairs echoing on the now uncarpeted treads. I clasped hold of discarded piece of wood from the flagstone floor, about the size and weight of a baseball bat, and quietly made my way up the stone steps to the hallway and settled in the shadows by the kitchen door, resting the wooden club on my shoulder.

**

Dr Carling looked up from the manuscript and stared into the space between herself and me, then without saying anything looked down again and continued to read the diary. I speculated as to her unsaid thoughts but didn't interrupt.

**

I wondered whether he had realized that there was someone else in his presence, hiding, waiting for the retreat away from danger. Like the knock on the door that you are trying to avoid. It gets louder and louder, angrier and more persistent. You press yourself into the shadows hardly able to breath for fear of discovery. Will he go away so that you can feel safe again. However, that is not how I react. Something inside my head dissipates the feeling of fear almost simultaneously with my need to extract justice and revenge.

'Hello?' I shouted from the shadows. The man turned and started forward, raising his fists, I immediately recognized Sally's description of Parsons, small, thin with a black moustache.

'Parsons?' Anger gripped me as I swung the raised wood with all my strength downwards towards his head. The ferocity of the blow surprised me as blood coursed down his face, his knees buckled, and he fell to the floor. I stood over his prostrate body, feeling calm despite the sight what I'd just done. I reached inside his blood-soaked jacket and took out his wallet, Graham R Parsons. I saw him stir and his eyes flickered open, and he began to raise his head. I dropped his wallet and pushed his head down with my hands firmly around his neck and learnt over him and whispered in his ear.

'I'm glad you came calling. Sally and Abbie have escaped your clutches forever, you miserable piece of shit.'

He spat at me and tried to wriggle free, but he wasn't a strong man. I held him and stuffed his tie down his throat and his scarf over his nose increasing the pressure, preventing him from taking any further breaths. His violent struggles began to subside. Oxygen starved blood was entering his brain as I pressed harder. I was now Sally Trimble extracting her revenge. His mind was becoming confused, dizziness was setting in, I felt him slip into unconsciousness. After a minute of continued pressure, his body became still, the blood from his head wound stopped flowing, but I still pressed both hands over his nose and mouth counting away the seconds, then the minutes. I knew then that the damage inside his head to the brain stem and cerebellum, were irreversible, his state, vegetative. I was still willing his other vital organs to start their inevitable chain of shutdown as they failed in death. I suddenly realized that I had been pressing down on him for fifteen minutes and relaxed my grip. My arms were numb from the effort, I was exhausted but elated now that justice had been done.

I bent over him. Why did I use the word "him"? He was no longer a living person. It was a dead body but still I was unable to refer to "it" as an inanimate object. It just didn't feel right.

As Graham Parsons lay on the hall carpet, I now had to think very carefully to make sure his death went unnoticed. 150,000 people go missing each year in Britain. He was about to become another statistic. I had to assume that no-one would have known that he come to 3 Burlington Avenue. It was unlikely that he had mentioned his affair to anyone and had just made another excuse for his absence from home. I also concluded that he would have entered Burlington Avenue surreptitiously avoiding being noticed. Now my task was to get his body into the basement and hidden before his muscular tissues became rigid. I didn't fancy having to break his bones to fit him into the temporary hiding place I envisaged. I had about three hours before rigor mortis set in, plenty of time.

Unlike my other dispatches, the Graham Parsons one was unplanned, but his unexpected arrival here relieved me of meticulous planning that I had briefly alluded to when I told Sally Trimble to "leave it to me", a few days ago. He had crossed her and my line. He had to go.

The old hall carpet was an ideal vehicle for conveying him down the stone steps into the basement. I rolled it around him and pulled it towards to open door. I thought it was unfortunate that he couldn't feel anything as his head followed his limp body as it banged against each step as we descended, finally coming to rest on the stone floor with a final crack. I wrenched open the cupboard and bungled Graham Parsons inside and closed the door, I was grateful that he was a small man otherwise I would have had difficulty in finding a suitable temporary resting place.

Time was now not on my side. Whilst the outward visible signs of death were very limited at the moment, under the surface of his skin the structural integrity of his cells throughout his body were beginning to break down, albeit slowly. His internal organs had already started to decompose. This gave me three or four days to find a permanent resting place, after that the build-up of gases would start to bloat his body with blood foam seeping from his mouth and nose. If I had not completed his grave by the end of the week, the neighbours would be experiencing unpleasant smells and swarms of flies emanating from 3 Burlington Avenue, London and I'd be in big trouble.

**

On the journey home I had been contemplating various way of disposal and had arrived at what I thought was a unique solution. I had heard of a panic sweeping parts of the country concerning the adverse health effect of Radon gas causing cancer. Could I install a radon sump? The flooring in the basement had to be relayed to eradicate any rising damp and what better place for me to bury Graham Parsons.

Armed with the latest manufacturer's installation guidance leaflet, I returned to 3 Burlington very early on the Saturday morning dressed for a hard day's labour in my rather shabby boiler suit carrying an electric jack hammer, extra lighting, shovels and stout sacks. I locked the basement door from the inside against prying eyes, then measured out the Radon sump void that was to be vented through external pipework at the rear up to roof level to extract the subterranean radon gas. The compacted mixture of earth and clay was easy to dig and within an hour I had removed sufficient to house the sump and quite a bit extra to accommodate Graham Parsons and the trench for the pipework to the outer wall. Outside I was pleased to see that the new guttering and white pipes had been secured to the rear of the building and extended into the basement.

I checked the locked cupboard, worried that Parsons was deteriorating faster than I had calculated but all seemed well, the carpet was doing its job and absorbing the small amount of escaping fluids.

I lowered the sump into position and connected the outside vent pipe, then unlocked the cupboard and dragged the carpet towards the grave. On the edge I unfurled it and let Graham Parsons roll into hole. The body slithered over the edge and with a squelching sound and came to rest on the hardcore against one of the open-air spigots. "Damn", I swore under my breath and jumped into the hole and dragged Parsons far enough away, but his clothes rose up and his skin ruptured. I was not ready for the smell of rotting meat tinged with a couple drops of cheap perfume. Despite my mask and gloves, I let go and wretched.

After several minutes I gathered my senses and returned to the present. I backfilled the surround area with hardcore and laid the heavy Radon resisting membrane over the whole floor ready for Ron to lay the concrete first thing on Monday, then I drove home. My thoughts returned to the horrific odour I had encountered earlier, but couldn't shake the smell away, I imagined his body turning from green to red, his blood decomposing, trying to bloat under the weight of his hardcore tomb as the gases began to rupture his corpse, the smell and gases being vented through new pipework into the London air as the wind passed over the roof of 3 Burlington Avenue.

A few weeks later with my Agent, in the basement, now full of light from the doors leading into the garden with the flagstones re-laid and polished, my eyes settled on Parsons' grave. I couldn't help imagining watching his nails and teeth beginning to fall from his body as it gradually turned to fluid. The smell would gradually dissipate as all that would remain as time passed would be cartilage and bone, allowing the real purpose of the sump to begin, removing Radon gas, if any. There was an air of tranquility in this mausoleum.

**

Dr Barbara Carling looked across the space between them provided by the small coffee table.

'Sorry to mention it but are you feeling up to this session? You look a little worse this week, if I'm being honest.'

'It's not been a good week, if I'm truthful. Seem to have lost some of my appetite although I do try to snack much of the time. Cannot contemplate sitting down for a large lunch or dinner. I've been told this is what I'm to expect. I try to keep drinking although this is beginning to be a chore, as well. Anyway, I'm fine really as long as you keep me topped up with tea and sweet biscuits whilst I'm here.'

Right on cue, her secretary entered and placed a cup of tea and a plate of chocolate biscuits in front of us.

'Thank you.'

I took a bit of a biscuit and a mouthful of tea to ease the swallowing.

'OK, I'm ready.' I looked at the red diary in her hand. She had paused to make little notes whilst reading through my latest confessional.

'What if Mr. Parsons hadn't come into the house whilst you were there? You said you held intractable ill-feelings towards him. Am I right?'

'From the first moment I listened to Sally Trimble's sad tale, I wanted him dead. I wanted to rid the world of a vile human being. The opportunity arose and then the planning set in. I am in no doubt that I would have found another way, if he hadn't walked in on me that night.'

'This may sound strange, but I'm sure you'll understand why I'm asking. You were alone unprepared in a dark basement at the time Parsons entered unannounced into your world. What fear do you recall, and do you remember linking it to your past?'

'Somehow, I knew it was him. I had always suspected he had obtained a key somehow without Sally knowing. As I turned off the torch and stood there listening, I remember the darkness became chilling, I clutched my head with both hands like the clamping forceps, turning to avoid the nick of the scalpel. These are feeling that I try to avoid. I run away from them as much as I can, like running across the ploughed field. In this case avoidance was impossible. I had to do something urgently to regain control of myself.'

'Did you realise that such feelings or thoughts had to be banished to deal with the present?'

'As soon as I confronted him, I felt fearless. Is that what you mean?"

'Perhaps. Did you recognize that the freedom from fear was unusual? Had you experienced that before?

In the moments before the deaths of Harris and the Headmaster, I had that same feeling and, incidentally the thoughts of over-elaboration, too much air, too much time, pass briefly through my mind but didn't mention these to Dr Carling. She could read about these later, so I just said.

'I think so. Anyway, to answer your question. The unpleasant emotion caused by the coming of danger just evaporated. Maybe here it lasted until after I had struck him and was hovering over his body, but those feelings dissipated almost immediately as I started to exert pressure, trying to prevent him from breathing. The chill had gone, and I was standing in a new situation that I had created. I felt the adrenalin pumping. Looking back, I think that's what induced me to over-indulge, pressing down on his face much longer than necessary to cause death, and "yes" to experiencing that before,' was all I could say.

'How did you feel kneeling over Parsons' body?'

'I'd overcome a threat, as I perceived it at the time. I felt satisfied, rewarded.'

'Anything else?'

'Relief as well. I had already made up my mind to extract revenge for Sally and Abbie. I was seeking justice for them. I remember telling him that at the time. He had deeply traumatized them both by his violence and I suppose I knew about traumatization myself and understood how damaging it could become, even a lifetime sentence. I never got to know whether there were other victims in his past, but I was pretty certain Sally and Abbie wouldn't have been the last and probably were not the first. There would be others in the future and once violence takes hold it usually escalates as time passes.'

'What I am having trouble with is why you have this underlying need to take matters into your own hands.'

'I suffered from knowing what was happening to me in a situation where I had no control in those first few minutes of my life. I could do nothing about the situation I was in. I was totally vulnerable. If you've never been there, felt it, smelled it and listened, you can never know how traumatic it is. So, to me, it is simple to answer your question. Parsons had committed Sally and Abbie to his prison. They had to leave behind their own needs so long as he had control over them in order to survive, but when I came along, they committed the future to me. I had no choice but to assist in that survival.'

'You became their refuge. Don't you think that is a convenient theory to hang your hat on for your actions? Most of us would have taken the conventional option; report the matter to the police and social services to deal with.'

'Not at all. If you could have seen them after it became known that Parsons was missing, then presumed dead, you would have been amazed how the fear, the memories of the past, the sleepless nights gradually vanished as they rebuilt their lives. They are still tenants of mine. Sally has a full-time job, Abbie at school, a complete turn-around of their lives has taken place. I felt justified that they'd trusted me and rebuilding their lives gave me great satisfaction.'

Chapter 10

Present Day - The Royal Oak London

This was Mike Randell's third meeting with Albert. He had reported to Roger Simmons and discussed the possibility of someone in the Garth Richards law firm being responsible for the death of Penfold. He had also questioned the reliability of his source of that information. Roger had advised him to proceed with caution. Mike was trying to understand how Albert was connecting Brian Simkins to his MI6 colleague's death. It seemed, so far, a tenuous thread woven by Albert's obsession with this man. He decided that he needed to draw as much as he could from Albert. Let him do the talking, but first, he needed to know why Albert was so convinced that Simkins was responsible for Albert's dismissal from the force.

'What was the evidence you had?' asked Mike.

'Brian was very righteous about domestic violence cases. In general, we had spoken a lot about police involvement or the lack of it in his eyes, more than I thought usual for an outsider, so I started to dig. In my own time I hasten to say. I did something stupid, looking back. I wanted a search warrant for one of his houses. Someone had gone missing, and I felt something bad had happened. The evidence was very circumstantial, but it did point to a house that Simkins had owned.

'Let me guess, you went there without a warrant.'

'Yep. My superiors found out and, well here I am.'

'What made you so suspicious apart from the timeline?'

'The alterations. Why fit a Radon sump in an area where there is no known gas prevalent?'

There was silence between them. Each thinking what was under that floor.

Albert fumbled in his inside pocket hidden by the overly large roll-neck sweater and pulled out several sheets of typed paper and handed them to Mike.

'Read these, no scan through them. I won't be long. Need to make a private call,' he said looking at his watch.

Mike took the sheets and started to read. By the time Albert returned he was on the last page. He lingered over the last few lines, wondering how Albert had obtained such detailed information. That question would come later. Mike bundled the sheets together and offered them back.

'No, keep them. I have a copy and some other interesting information about our Mr Simkins. Anyway, as I recall you wanted my help, Michael, you wanted to talk about the late Mr Penfold.'

'The explosion and death of Penfold. He was one of our own, Albert. Afraid I can't tell what he was investigating.'

'I already know the answer, Michael. Fraud and money laundering.'

Mike was surprised by the statement. There was nothing in the press and certainly nothing would have leaked from MI6's offices. Albert was extremely well informed by someone.

'I won't either confirm or deny, Albert. Nevertheless, I have been ordered to find out who killed him and that is why I am here, even at this late stage. We don't like loose ends.'

'So, you need my help.'

'Yes, but not officially as yet.'

'Okay. What is your email address? Private, Michael. Cell phone would help as well. Know how you guys travel.'

Chapter 11

The Management Consultant

Session 3

I relaxed into the settee and took a tentative sip of tea and opened my brief case and extracted a diary and handed it to Dr Carling. She opened it and started to read the first sentence.

Following the clear upset and disruption caused by Adrian Penfold, I decided that it should be me to take hold of the situation and resolve the problems he was creating.

'Brian. Can you explain before I read on exactly what disruption you are referring to?'

'Barbara, it will become apparent if you read on but as you've asked, and to put it simply, that man was prying into every corner of my department at Garth Richards during valuable working hours. Stopping the flow of work, asking for a copy of this or that procedure. When you are working to tight schedules these interviews can wait until after hours or indeed ask me, not my staff.'

'I see. I'll read on.'

**

Some years ago, one evening at my office, after the support staff had left and Penfold had departed in very much of a hurry and ran down the corridor, checking his watch as if he was late for an out-of-hours meeting. I used my partners' pass key that gave me access through the first barrier of his domain and into his office. I sat at his desk, foolishly he'd left his computer in sleep mode and forgotten to turn it off completely in his hurry to leave.

It took a few moments to bring his machine to life and then to find his file on the firm. A prompt came up "Do you want another copy?". I searched the drawers of his desk, just in case he'd left the copy in his office. Nothing. Maybe he had taken it with him in a hurry for what? I dismissed the thought for the moment. I put in my flash drive and downloaded what I needed. Turned off the computer and locked his office, leaving no trace of my intrusion. At home I downloaded the contents of the flash drive. What I read was very disturbing and I began to feel a rage within. It seemed clear to me that he was not a Management Consultant at all, but a Forensic Accountant. Did anyone in the firm suspect? I was sure that no one knew actually knew that he was connected to MI5 and MI6. Thoughts of disbarment and prison raced through my mind.

His recommendations, based on analysis on the international money trail within the firm's bank accounts, suggested that all the senior partners, including myself must have been complicit and thus under the principle of collective responsibility, be the subject of criminal charges. His intention was to find enough evidence to prosecute some of my partners. My department was mentioned as a possible vehicle for laundering money through property transactions. How long would it be before Administrators were brought in? I also knew that all our department transactions would bear very close scrutiny. Nevertheless, the commercial evidence that was contained in those pages, would bring down the firm and my life's work would have been ripped away from under my feet and I be tarred with the same brush whatever happened. Personally, I could not let that happen as I was looking forward to retirement and an easier life. The thought of financial ruin, bankruptcy and years of court cases was unconscionable.

I started to imagine squeezing Adrian Penfold's neck with my hands, watching his eyes bulge and his face redden. Lifting the little figure-crunching accountant off his feet and watching him fumbling with his tie as he pulled himself from the floor. I cast the images aside. He was not going to get away with this, I resolved.

I had this crazy notion that November the fifth seemed like a fitting date. It was three weeks away, enough time if I planned it properly.

I finished the scotch and retired to bed. I kept thinking of Guido Fawkes in his failed attempt to blow up the Houses of Parliament in the name of Catholicism and in revenge for Protestant persecution. Leaving religion aside and despite my several whiskies, sleep didn't come easily; too many ideas floating around. Get rid of the fantastic ones, concentrate on the real possibilities. The following morning, instead of going straight to the office, I decided to carry out my first reconnaissance of Adrian Penfold's residence.

I turned off the main road in West Hampstead and drove towards his house at No. 33. I stopped the car opposite. A nice sqwat detached Edwardian residence, newish UPVc windows. On closer inspection, I was pleased to see that they did not incorporate any air trickle vents at the top. I was not unhappy to see that the navy-blue front door had a larger than normal letterbox, no doubt installed to allow larger packages to be delivered without disturbance. On either side there was a lawned area with neatly trimmed high hedges dividing it from its neighbour, which was good for what was developing in my mind. I wandered down the road. At the end of the road was a patch of grassland with wood stacked high in a pyramid and set to one side was an area that I assumed from various metal constructions was going to be for the pyrotechnic display. Yellow printed signs announced the time of the festivities which I noted down. At this time of day, I was reasonably sure no-one had seen me or bothered to take notice of my car. In fact, the street was deserted.

How memorable a special Guy Fawkes night was going to be depended on the next few days as

I disappeared after dinner into my shed in the garden.

The firework I bought is a concentrate of flash powder. I was at pains to ensure that mine was a single paper tube containing potassium perchlorate and aluminium powder and some sulphur to increase sensitivity. The one I had chosen had a very fast burning fuse. I was told it would produce a very loud bang, so my timing had to be perfect that night.

I gingerly placed the tube on the table in my shed and covered it with a sheet. Now for the second part of my plan without which my "airbomb" would be useless. I had always been fascinated by disasters and how they were caused. I needed to know exactly what happened and who was responsible. It seemed to be a catalogue of small errors leading to the catastrophe whether on the day or in the flawed design, or both. And so, it was that lying awake with the whiskey still coursing through my body that my thoughts turned to another disaster which ultimately led me to my current plan.

You may recall that on 6 May 1937, the German airship, Hindenburg, a leviathan of its age, a glittering example of science, engineering and passenger luxury making the Atlantic Ocean crossing from Europe much quicker than the fleet of opulent ships. On that particular day, it was attempting to land, after crossing the Atlantic from Frankfurt, at Lakehurst Naval Airstation,

New Jersey. Bad weather had slowed its progress, but by the time it had made its first pass over Lakehurst, the poor weather conditions began to improve and Captain Pruss made a tight turn to line up with the mooring mast. It was usual practice for the massive airship to drop a mooring cable and landing ropes and be winched down to the mooring mast. Unknown to all inside the control room and passenger lounges, one of the hundreds of taut cable bracers at the stern near the tailfin had snapped inside the gigantic fuselage during the Captain's too tight a turn and had ruptured one of the hydrogen bags that gave the craft lift, However the bracing cable was still flying around within the superstructure. The massive airship had attracted a huge load of static electricity from flying close to the storm which would normally be earthed through the ropes and cables used in landing, but the charge remained within the airship as the ropes and cables were wet and unable immediately to act as earthing for the static. Whilst hydrogen is an inflammable gas, it needs a source to ignite it. It will not ignite on coming into contact with the air as it was escaping through the canvas skin but the combination of the static electricity and a spark from broken cable ignited the whole craft and in less than forty seconds, it became a smouldering wreck of twisted metal, killing 36 people. In my case I reflected that my target was one man and I had calculated that I had less than a minute to achieve success.

The first part of the plan was lying on my bench in front of me, the "explosive spark" in my course of action. What I needed now was to introduce the catalyst element that would end Penfold's ruinous ideas that he'd outlined in his Report. Was this personal mission of mine to permanently rid Garth Richards of this man, a step too far? I dismissed the thought, after all there were other jobs at risk. I was fighting for them as well. I decided that I had enough evidence to persuade those partners who knew about their criminality to retire quietly after Penfold's demise.

I needed access to Penfold's house. My observations at various times of visiting the Hawthorns led me to believe that he was not a fresh air addict as I had never seen any of his windows open to the elements and at night, they were heavily curtained. I decided early on that breaking-in was not necessary as on my daytime morning passes, I had noticed that his house was visited by an elderly lady who let herself in. Did he have a cleaning lady? If so, that was my passport for entry

At my desk in the office, various disguises floated in and out of my mind, then remembering the ID chain in my drawer, I took it out and removed the card attached. It wasn't difficult to create a new one using the office photocopier and an old photograph I always kept in my wallet. To complete my disguise, I needed a dark blue cap and woollen worsted suit, then, I hoped it would be acceptable to the elderly cleaning lady.

It was now that I really started to question what I was doing and the immense lengths to which I was going. Was I now on an unstoppable treadmill that I had created for myself? The more elaborate my plan became, the more clues I would leave exposed for the subsequent investigation. I had never, in the past, felt as fearful as now. I stood in front of the mirror, looking at myself for several minutes. Was I becoming a victim of my own creation of survival techniques? Penfold was just doing the job that he had been asked to undertake. Was I, a married man with two late teenage children, just a fucked-up soul that could not escape from his past? A jigsaw of many pieces that fitted together perfectly most of the time, but when turned upside down, in this case by Penfold, became impossible to what? Act in a just and fair way? Overlook his threat to me and others? Ignore the trauma I felt from within? The more I questioned what I was proposing, the more virtuous I became and that it was the right thing to do.

Three days later, November 4, I stood looking down Greenlip Road; no.33 was towards the middle. I felt nervous, imagining faces peering from behind curtains, whispered voices, pointing fingers. I adjusted the clipboard in my hand and tightened the grip on the yellow box containing various dials and pipes. These had been purchased from an electrical wholesaler near Marble Arch and adapted in my shed to look authentic. I walked down the path and pressed the bell of no.33 and waited. My woollen suit was itching by now as I fumbled to relieve the irritation. My glasses began to mist over as I heard a machine being silenced and footsteps descend the stairs and approach the door, I hurriedly replaced them, half cleaned.

'We've had a call today about a possible gas leak. I'm checking several houses,' I said mimicking my early Liverpool accent that was never far from my normal voice. I put on a pair of gloves indicating I needed to come inside. 'I have to check there are no defects with each installation.'

I lifted the yellow box a little closer for her to see. This settled it, as she opened the door wider to let me pass inside.

'Don't let me interrupt you."

'Well, you have, haven't you?' she said rather abruptly as I rested my hand on the banister encouraging her to resume her hoovering upstairs. She took the first step, looked at me, and continued upwards, barking over her shoulder. 'Mind you don't dirty any of my floors.'

Ahead of me was the open door to the kitchen to one side of the house overlooking a gardened area and had open doors into the rear sitting room with TV. I set down the yellow box and uncoiled the length of hose. The gas range was an old version but gleamed as if it had never been used and, perfect for my purposes, was connected by a flexible gas pipe. I turned the key to the back door and eased it open as slowly and quietly as I could. I stopped and listened, the hoover had moved on and was in a room over my head. Outside, the gas meter box was hidden behind an overgrown shrub still supporting some delicate red flowers. I brushed it aside and closed the valve to "off". I looked along the side path towards the road and then up at the adjacent neighbouring first floor windows. They were frosted glass, so no chance of being seen unless they were opened whilst I was outside. I returned to the kitchen silently closing the door and locking it. A few turns of the securing nut and the range supply was partially disconnected. I could smell the mercaptan additive to the colourless, odourless lethal domestic gas supply. I wafted away with my hands the acrid smell of rotten eggs.

'Hello, I shouted up the stairs. 'I'm off now but I need to talk to you.'

The whine of the hoover motor subsided as she came down the stairs. I looked at my clipboard for comfort and in a serious tone of many years of legal training.

'What's that awful smell?

'The gas I was talking about.' I said, 'Mr. Penfold's range is dangerous. I've put some tape across the top as a reminder that it must not be used until it is properly serviced and made safe.' I adjusted my glasses and opened the door to let myself out.

I left Greenlip Road for the penultimate time, walking to where I had parked the car some half a mile away. I stripped the handmade ID and ripped it into small pieces before discarding them into various waste bins, throwing away one glove here, another there and my glasses and cap elsewhere. The gasman had disappeared.

The next day, 5 November, I was dressed like a hobo with an old bobble hat, matching scarf and shabby waxed jacket as I set off for Greenlip Road. My assumption that Perkins would avoid the celebrations at the end of his road were confirmed as I glanced to my left and saw him bathed in bright light in the kitchen drinking from a wine glass. All the other houses appeared to be in darkness, no doubt their occupants congregating around the glowing bonfire further down.

I stopped outside No. 31. The road was deserted and calm apart from the noise coming from the Guy Fawkes celebrations. I was relying on timing being my companion and friend as I ducked down and ran towards the gas tap of Perkins' house at No. 33. I imagined the slight hiss in his kitchen as the explosive vapour began to fill the room. I had a clear view of Perkins' head resting on the cushions and the flickering screen of the TV in front of him. On the side table next to him was an empty wine glass and upturned bottle in the cooler. Had he fallen asleep? That would be an added bonus.

I fingered the airbomb and lighter tucked into the folds of my jacket. I looked at my watch, the display start time was moments away. I waited. The first rockets thrust into the sky at the end of the street and burst into crackling colours. I lit the long fuse and thrust it through Penfold's letterbox.

I made my way down the road and towards the toffee apple stand at the end. I had not eaten toffee apples for years, so I bought one. As I took our first bite, it was a reminder of years ago shortly after Annie and I first met. I was about to take another lump out of the apple when the display we were watching was overshadowed by an enormous boom. All of us stopped and looked up Greenlip Road. Flames were leaping out of no. 33 where the downstairs window frames hung in ruins clinging to the blackened brickwork. Everything stopped, no one moved. Only the crackle of the bonfire could be heard above the shocked silence, then panic set in as people stumbled over each other and ran up the road. The Guy Fawkes evening was immediately abandoned. Minutes later the wailing sirens of the fire trucks were heard in the distance. The shrill sound of the ambulance was first on the scene. All the medics could do was watch and wait. The house was a burning wreck as smoke billowed into the still night air.

Having observed the devastation my handiwork had caused and in the certain knowledge that Perkins had perished inside, I moved away from the gawping crowd and through the side streets away from Greenlip Road.

**

Dr Barbara Carling put my papers on the coffee table and looked across at me. I sipped my coffee and gazed back at her. The silence in those few moments was overwhelmingly shocking and horrifying. It was me who couldn't believe what I had done. I had understood why I had done it but… She interrupted my silent thoughts.

'This is pretty horrifying, Brian.'

Her statement was expected but not the delivery, the way in which she spoke. Where did her sympathies lie? For me, or Penfold. I wasn't sure.

'What kind of image do you, did you, have of this man, Adrian Penfold?'

I rocked back against the seat cushions and gazed at the ceiling trying to pick the right words. I had a physical picture of him in my mind but that was not going to be enough.

'He was a little shit. He was working undercover, watching, lying, had no emotional or spiritual attachment to what he was proposing to do.'

She could see I, her patient, was still very emotionally attached to these events.

'Did it not occur to you that he was just doing his job and that your attitude was totally irrational not to say, murderous?'

'You never met him. He was not evil, I'm not saying that, but he was destitute of empathy for others. If his financial forensics proved others were solely responsible, his mind was made up, no thoughts of the effect on the innocents whose lives would have been devastated.'

'Couldn't you have worked with him once you discovered what he was up to, worked out a compromise?'

'No!' That was all I could say. I had questioned my motives already, but now I began to realise that perhaps there was another way that I had not considered.

'What happened in the end? Nobody ever question you? Thought that you may be involved?"

'We were all interviewed by the police. The Coroner concluded that the cause of death was accidental, caused by a faulty gas cooker and that the absence of smoke inhalation meant he had died before the explosion and the destruction of his house. He was poisoned by the gas leak. His alcohol blood levels were high. There were some unanswered questions as to how the gas ignited but the devastation inside was too great to be certain of the cause. As to his undercover work, mysteriously, that never came to light.'

'What happened to his housekeeper?'

'She told the police about the faulty gas range. I think this was the clincher as far as the Coroner's verdict was concerned, despite never being able to locate the bespectacled inspector. I have to confess that I was surprised the police didn't attach more significance to this part of the puzzle, but as they could apparently find no motive for foul play, perhaps they decided not to pursue this line of enquiry. They had no known relatives or close friends to satisfy.'

'As a matter of interest what did you do with the evidence?'

'Early retirement for a couple of partners and I decided to join them soon afterwards.

'No Penfold's report, the copy he took the day you searched his office.'

'Never discovered what happened to it. A worrying loose end that I still wake up thinking about.'

Chapter 12

Mike Randell's Apartment Docklands East London

Mike opened Albert's electronic file and started to read, as it was printing out. Albert had set out a family history of Brian Simkins that he managed to research somehow. What was he looking for? The past quite often predicted the future, thought Mike.

It was now very clear to Mike that his assessment of Albert's state of mind when they had talked in the pub was correct. Albert's obsession with this man was verging on manic. He wanted revenge from all the bad things that had befallen him that he was convinced had been caused by Brian Simkins. As he flicked onto the next page it was clearly becoming a duel that one man knew about and the other, Simkins, was ignorant of. Mike needed all his objectivity to analyse what was real and what was supposition. He also wanted to know how Albert had obtained the detail which could not possibly have come from normal research. For the moment, he decided not to press that point. There would come a time when he would need the answer, but not now, although he knew from Albert's electronic file that he was dictating not typing. The algorithms of the speech recognition software were making heavy weather of some of the contents.

According to Albert, he had managed to persuade a former colleague, at an early stage, to keep him informed of progress in the investigation into the explosion resulting in the death of Mike's colleague, Penfold. "How?" didn't matter. Mike now accepted that Albert was, in truth, walking a tightrope between conventional policing and lawless behaviour. Ethics had been abandoned. Mike now had his hold over Albert even though he had no intention of exploiting it at the moment.

The transcript stated that the explosion had taken place on the 5 November, a Saturday. The contents of bins in the immediate surrounding area had been collected by Albert's former police colleagues as part of their investigation. He had accessed with the help of a former friend in the force, Sergeant John Deacon, the contents those bins. It had taken Albert two weeks of painstaking searching through the refuse to recover the discarded gloves, a name badge, and glasses He eventually gave all these back to the police. His private deal with forensics came up with a blank on fingerprints but there was some DNA that didn't apparently cross-reference with anybody on the database. Albert wasn't surprised at that development. He managed to have a chat to Penfold's weekly cleaning lady and put together a detailed picture of the gasman and managed to persuade her to identify some of the items he had recovered from the bins and a photograph of Brian Simkins. He was certain that the Coroner's verdict was incorrect, but he never divulged this mounting evidence he had unearthed to Sergeant Deacon. 'Why not?' asked Mike to himself. What was his ulterior motive, if not to see Simkins charged with Arson and Manslaughter, to name the two easy indictments. Was that not revenge enough?

Mike was beginning to worry about his association with ex-Detective Inspector Albert Thornton. Albert knew all the tricks and the people to carry them out. He had already admitted to using underhand methods to find out more about Simkins' former rented house and now this. Again, Mike decided to bide his time.

Mike was wrestling with the problem when realised the time. He was meant to be at Heathrow to meet Hillary in an hour.

'You look a wreck, Mike.' Her first words came as no surprise, he felt a wreck.

'Thanks. Good to see you too. Actually, you look gorgeous, Ms Barnes.' He stepped back to admire her, then leaped forward to hug her tightly. 'Am I forgiven for looking a wreck,' he whispered in her ear.

'Of course, you silly man.'

He grabbed her case and they walked hand in hand to the Heathrow Express station and then to

Mike's apartment. The sitting room table was littered with photographs, type-written pages and Mike's scrawled handwriting. He immediately gathered them into a bundle away from Hilary's eyes.

'Been busy, Mike?'

Mike knew he could trust Hilary implicitly now she'd signed the Official Secrets Act at Roger Simmons's insistence. She had helped him solve a series of murders of the Elridge family in Cairo last year.

His mind slipped back to the Sunday that he fell in love with her as they lazily drifted in a felucca down the Nile, only for him to ruin it all by not telling her their weekend away in Luxor was a trap to capture the man who was determined to torture and kill her. He knew he had made a terrible mistake in not confiding in her. It had taken all his humble apologies and expressions of devotion to bring her back into his life. He was determined not to make the same mistake again.

'Yes. I'll put these away. Coffee?' Instead, he left them on the table and walked into the open-plan kitchen. Watching her curiosity get the better of her as she lifted the first page, then the second, as he busied himself working the coffee machine.

As he returned to the table with two mugs, he set them down and reached across to the papers. Hilary put her hand on his arm.

'Want to talk about them?'

'Not after our last joint effort,' he laughed.

'I've forgiven you, Mike. You know that now, I hope. You did what you thought was right, at the time, despite nearly getting me killed in the process.'

He leaned forward and kissed her gently.

'Well?' Hilary picked up the first sheet and waved it in front of him. Mike sighed.

He told Hilary about the death of Penfold in the explosion, then the story of missing man, Graham Parsons.

'Interesting, this man Simpkins.'

'Certainly, he's in the frame, but I am seriously concerned about trusting Albert. He seems to be treading a fine line between what is lawful and what is not now he's no longer a policeman.'

'Michael, that's what you do all the time in your job. Isn't it?'

'We have more covert operators that's for certain and the protection of the Foreign Office if we need it, but we still have to work within the rule of law.'

'I thought you were only responsible for overseas operations. What you've said so far looks like domestic to me.'

'It is both. Despite our protectiveness and inherent distrust of MI5, they were brought in to help us identify some London commercial customers they had under suspicion for money laundering so coupled with our foreign intelligence, we sent in Penfold to do some forensic accounting at the same firm where Simkins is a partner.'

'And so, you came into contact with Albert to see what he knew?'

'Yes, I approached him. He set me onto Simkins and I asked him to send me what he had on the man.' Mike picked up the papers as evidence.

'I was reading them and lost track of time, then realised I had to pick you up.'

'Thence the wreck that met me.' Hilary smiled that smile that lit up her whole face. He'd been attracted by its innocence.

'OK, while I shower, you're welcome to read if you want. I'm sure you are cleared to this level.'

'Try and stop me. I cannot help unless I know what there is in this lot.' Hilary began to read ex-DI Albert Thornton's treatise.

Chapter 13

Mike' Apartment same day

Hilary then started to read Albert's next type-written evidence marked "The Bully", but after the first few sentences stopped. Looking out of the floor length glass at nothing in particular, she agreed with Mike. This passage of writing could only have been obtained by illegal surveillance. Who was using who? Was Albert using Mike or vice versa. Hillary was convinced Mike needed to be very careful.

**

'How did you feel as the train left the platform? You were only six and a quarter years old, Brian.' said Dr Carling.

He could feel the concern of someone other than a professional in her voice, more like a mother afraid for the safety of one of her children. He looked at her for a moment a little unsure of the exact words to describe the feelings he had at the time.

'Feel? 'What had I done wrong to deserve this?'

'Were you happy before that train journey?'

'Most of the time. Yes, I was happy, Barbara.'

'Can you remember the times when you were not happy?'

'When I couldn't understand why I wasn't allowed to see my father when he was ill. I was unhappy then.'

'Your father. Can you tell me about him?'

'He disappeared from my life just before my third birthday.'

'Disappeared? That is an unusual description.'

'Well, that is how it felt. One day, my mother told me that 'Daddy was unwell' and had gone to Clatterbridge Hospital for some tests. She gave me a train and some track to push about that my father had asked her to buy for me. I never saw him again. He never came home to give me a hug. My mother went to visit him for months. I was never allowed to go with her.'

'Do you know why?'

'I've thought about that many times, over the years. As you know the two world wars had brought horrors on an unimaginable scale. These affected my mother's parents and then my mother. I think the prevailing philosophy in the family was to keep me away from more tragedy, keep me happy, there'd been too much grieving and as a three year old, I wouldn't have understood what was happening. I don't know. The tragedy is that I would have understood. He had an infectious disease, maybe they were advised to keep me away. I never raised the subject with my mother. Just one of the many questions that I wished I had asked before she developed senile dementia. Anyway, he was encased in an iron-lung machine.

Polio had caused paralysis of his diaphragm and the intercostal muscles essential for breathing. Maybe seeing my father with his whole body encased in this mechanical negative pressure ventilator, just his head free at one end, they believed the awful vision of which would have stayed with me forever and given me nightmares on a grand scale. Particularly the sound of the bellows artificially changing the air pressure inside pulling air into his lungs and then allowing them to fall again, minute after minute, day in day out. It would have been the sight and the noise that would have stayed with me.'

'Do you think they were right?'

'Let's just say that I understand that decision now. They wanted to preserve my image of him as a Dad which is exactly what happened albeit with limited memories for our short time together. What I cannot forgive, is not being able to say 'goodbye'. I should have been allowed to go to the funeral. I'm not sure what it would have given me but maybe finality in some sense that I could process.

'Unusually, I think I would have understood the finality of death even at that age. It was as if "big boys don't cry". It was only much, much later in life that I was able to break out of hiding my feelings which had been suppressed since his death, but even now I find some situations too difficult and hide away.'

'So, did you expect to see him again?'

'I used to tell myself, he'll be back soon, and we'd be a family again. A lot of fuss was made of me by my grandparents, uncles and aunts. They were there to keep my mind away from negative feelings and thoughts.'

'Did you ever feel angry that he was no longer around.'

'Yes, I was angry at times, but I don't know where that anger was directed. I think if he had left or taken his own life, then it would have been directed at him, but I don't recall that it was. I just felt desperately let down, I suppose.'

**

Hillary called Mike from bedroom. 'How much of this have you read Mike?'

'I scanned most of it. Why?'

'To me it looks like your friend, Albert, has been listening and recording these very private conversations. It's written as if a bugged conversation and he has somehow copied the diaries as well. Do you have any idea who this Barbara is?'

'No. Not at the moment. Albert has been very cagey about his sources.'

'Cagey is the wrong word, Mike. It seems to me he does not trust you, yet?'

'I know but remember the more of this stuff he gives me the greater he has to trust me because he knows every piece of personal information he divulges to me about Simkins gives me the legal edge against him. Anyway, the lack of trust is mutual, Hillary,' shouted Mike above the noise of the hair drier.

'Okay, I am curious about this man, Simkins. Let me read on.'

**

'Can I ask you when you started to read?'

'Read?' What has this got to do with anything, Barbara?'

'I don't know yet. Maybe nothing but I need a full picture, Brian.'

'Okay. Before I went to school, yes, well before.'

'So what age were you and what happened at school?'

'I am not really sure when I started reading simple words in books. At my first school after they had discovered that I could read, I was put at the back of the class away from the rest and given real stories and illustrated history and science books and the occasional one to one with the teacher who pushed me onto more difficult language concepts."

'Did that make you feel different or isolated?'

'Yes, and yes, but it didn't bother me. I enjoyed the challenge. No, that's not quite true. I found I didn't have too many friends I could relate to, of my own age.'

'Is that where the title of this diary came from?' She waved the papers at me. I stared at the words 'The Bully'.

'That's where it started but it didn't last long. I wasn't the only one. The fat boy from my class took the brunt of the bullying from the older boys. I was taller than most but really skinny. Unsupervised free time in the playground was the time I didn't look forward to as one particular boy thought kicking people was a great sport and I succumbed to his attention on many occasions.'

'Did you respond?'

'No. I was no fighter. I just took the punishment and stood there. I found that eventually, with no reaction, he'd give up. It was a victory for me despite the bruising.

'What did your mother say about the bruising? What did you say?

'Usual explanation. I fell over or was pushed when we played games. She was never more inquisitive, and I wasn't going to be a sneak or considered a weakling. It was then that I promised myself that when I could, I would never let anyone get away with plunging my sensitive emotions into turmoil. If I was confronted with unfairness or injustice at those sorts of level, I would find a way to get even.'

'So, let me get this clear in my mind. Are you telling me that you alone, even at your tender age, were to be the arbiter of what is unfair and or unjust within the confines of your life?'

'Yes. I realise that may sound very strange and is subjective but not in my mind. I am sure you have come across juveniles that have already made their minds up about what they believe in and how they propose to deal with those beliefs. Why not someone who is younger having the same feelings?'

'Do you tolerate arrogance?'

'Before I answer that, Barbara. Let me say that I have since those early days never wavered from the same premise. History tells us, at least history written by the victors, that eventually they succumb to the very ends they seek to instill on others. Justice is a pretty good arbiter in the final analysis. Unfairness has a habit of rebounding back to the perpetrator in the end.

'Anyway, back to your question about arrogance. The answer is unequivocally, not at all. It is a word that has subjective perspective. If someone has an intellect that is way above the norm, or a talent for music or painting that surpasses all others, some may say that their expression is a form of arrogance. Passing judgement on our fellow beings is also a form of arrogance. No, if I see something that is unfair or unjust, it would only be in the context of what others would perceive it to be and that would be justification enough, in my estimation.'

'Just to recap a moment, Brian, on something we discussed earlier in the first session together. I find it very difficult to conceive, from a medical perspective and what I've learned in my training, that anyone has a memory that extends into a pre-natal state without thinking that it might have been learned in retrospect.'

'So, I've been told. I've heard it all before. I know you was wrong. I've felt it, I feel it now as you look at me.'

'I'm trying to understand, in very unusual human developmental circumstances, what effect these early memories might manifest themselves in your continued growth through childhood to today, if any, as this is uncharted territory for me and, I suspect, most psychiatrists.'

'I'm afraid I cannot help you. Maybe as we progress……'

**

Hillary put down the papers as Mike breezed into the sitting room looking more like his vibrant self.

'How do I look?'

'Dishy!'

'Good. Ready for a stroll along the river?'

Hillary stood up and took his arm and walked to the door. They walked slowly along the tree-lined footpath until they turned into The Green Man. Having bought their drinks, they strolled into the garden and sat down.

'Right, tell me about Moscow. You've been very silent on the subject.'

'They've had enough of me. My contract ends next month and with it my tenure. I was going to mention it earlier, but your Mr Simkins got in the way.'

'What's next then?'

'Nothing at the moment, save unemployment.'

'Need a base? You can have the other bedroom as your personal space,' replied Mike knowing what the answer would be.

'Thank you, I'll bear that in mind.' A bashful smile crossed her face.

'Good that's settled then. So, what are your thoughts on the Simkins file?'

'It looks to me that our man is undergoing some personal journey, as if he's been struggling to understand who he is.'

'My take exactly. Why would someone at his age want to engage in self-analysis?'

'That question needs an answer, Mike.'

'Hang on a moment.' Mike pulled the mobile from his top pocket and pressed Albert's number.

'Albert, thanks for the file. I'm intrigued. How did you get the information?' Mike put it on speaker and Hilary leaned forward.

'I have my contacts, Mike.'

'I know your net spreads far and wide, but, if I may suggest, what I read seems to suggest you have….'

'Mike, I've been following this man for months. I know everywhere he goes, but not what he says. I needed something more, hence the listening device I had installed some weeks back. Trouble is it only does half the job. I have a man with a camera and at lot of. How shall I put it? Experience.'

'Albert, I don't want to hear the details.'

'Of course. I wouldn't have given you them, anyway, apart from answering your question.'

'Albert, this Barbara woman, who is she and why is he going there each week?'

'Good questions. Dr Barbara Carling is a highly regarded psychotherapist. As for why he goes there, I can only guess. Maybe he wants someone to listen to clear his conscience.'

'I think there's more to it than that, Albert. I'll do some checking, Albert, promise me you'll not do anything further until we speak again.'

'My word is my bond. I promise, and why should I. I think that I am getting what I want now. Time will tell.'

Mike turned off the phone and looked at Hilary for inspiration whilst finishing his beer.

'Another? Why not?' Hilary rose and took a pace towards bar and turned, ducked her head towards him and said, 'Advice, Mike. Steer very carefully with Albert. He could easily make a mistake that would rebound on you, me and MI6.'

'If I were honest, I think it's too late for that.'

Mike watched appreciatively as she strolled off carrying the two empty glasses and waited in thought for her return.

'Thanks,' said Mike as he sipped the ale from his glass. 'I worry that Albert has not been exactly helpful to the Penfold police investigation. That is my priority. In fact, the only reason I contacted Albert. He has obtained plenty of evidence. Yet kept it to himself. I'm already trying to distance myself, hence recording my instructions to lay off any further illegal intrusion in Carling's office.' He tapped his phone to confirm the statement.

'Good. There's more to Albert's motives than meets the eye. Can I make a suggestion?'

'You've not hesitated before.' He smiled mockingly.

'What's tomorrow? Friday. Yes. We will split our efforts, said Hillary. I'll try to find out why Simkins is undergoing these sessions now. And you?'

I will investigate his early past in West Wales.'

'Why Wales, Mike?

'Oh. You've not read the rest of the Session. I forgot. Read it when we get back. You will understand why.'

Mike took Hilary's hand as they wandered slowly back

Chapter 14

The Bully II

Session 4

Hillary would start her investigations into Dr Barbara Carling in the morning. She picked up the remaining sheets of paper that Albert's had sent through. She now knew she was handling information obtained by devious criminal means that were still ongoing. Totally unethical but nevertheless intriguing and, although she didn't want to admit it, exciting. It was the early years of Simkins, as the conversation between him and Dr Carling unfolded.

**

The year is not relevant only my age. I was ten years old. Three and a half years earlier, I was put on a train at Chester railway station in a carriage with a seat next to the guard's van. I remember hugging my mother briefly as she kissed me on my head and then we parted company as I was shepherded into that carriage by a large man with a comforting manner and endearing smile. I remember he was carrying a large green flag. I sat by the window watching the waving hand of my mother on the platform as the train began to move forward. As there was no-one around to see,

I managed a short wave back at her. I don't know why but I was never comfortable with feelings of emotion You know, love, kissing, hugging and expressing lovely sentiments. It had never really happened after I was born. Of course, I had been held closely, like all babies and young children but something was missing. I could feel it.

I could see my own reflection in the window. Blue cap perched on my head, matching blue blazer, white shirt, blue tie and grey short trousers. I looked down at my shiny black shoes. I felt a wave of embarrassment pass through me as if the whole world were looking at me and pointing. "Look at mummy's boy. Where's the father?".'

I hugged the tin box on my lap. Inside was a jam sandwich, a bar of Cadbury's chocolate and a glass bottle of orange juice sealed by a rubber ring with glass sprung stopper.

'How did you feel as the train left the platform?'

'Feel?' 'What had I done wrong to deserve this?'

'Were you happy before that train journey?'

'Most of the time. Yes, I was happy.'

'Umm, reliving the death of anyone is bad enough, but when it is your father, it is a hundred-fold greater.'

'Tell me more about that journey? These early memories are an important ingredient for my understanding.'

'Every bit?

'Yes. Every memory.'

The guard checked that I was still seated next to the window as the train gathered speed on its way south. To relieve the monotony of the uninteresting flat countryside that swept passed, I started counting the clack-clack of the wheels as they passed over the joints in the rails, checking the second hand on my new watch. My leaving present from my grandfather which I treasured for years, even though eventually I could no longer wind the mechanism to make it work, it remained on my wrist.

My obsession with obscure facts allowed me to calculate the increasing speed of the train. Each rail was a specific length and the number of times the wheels crossed the joints per minute gave the approximate speed of the train. By the time I reached sixty with the train rocking side to side, I decided that was fast enough. I have no idea where this odd fascination for facts comes from but tucked in my pocket was my bible of information; world's longest river, Amazon 3976 miles, highest mountain, Everest 29,029 feet, world's tallest man, Robert Wadlow 8 feet 11.1 inches and on it went. This little book kept me happy mile after mile, arithmetic formula and simple scientific theories, but then as always, the dark side of me surfaced. Why at this point I cannot tell. Something prompted it, an abstract observation on the pages, a shadow passing the train window, the whistle from the engine. I just cannot remember all the triggers. I start to feel anxious and alone. The future was beckoning, and I had no idea how to cope.

By the time I had finished my tin box of goodies, it was time to change trains. I was escorted with my tin box under my arm and my satchel swinging to and fro over my other arm into the waiting room and into the clutches of a rather short stout lady who introduced herself as the station-master's wife. I remember the conversation even now.

'Did you enjoy your journey? Are you looking forward to your new school? I hear it's near the seaside.'

'I managed a nod, I think.'

'Well, I'm sure you'll have a fine time. I'll be back shortly. Just wait here. Would you like a glass of milk?'

'I was parched and nodded enthusiastically but remained standing.'

'I'll be back in a jiffy.'

She left the door open. The smell of that railway station is always something that I'll remember. The timber, the paintwork, everything smelled of soot and coal. Every surface had been wiped down daily but still the aroma lingered in the air.

She returned and handed me the glass. I sat by the open door as the last rays of sun settled on my knees.

'How old are you?'

'Over six.'

'She nodded and left. I leaned forward and watched and listened.'

'Why would anyone send a lovely boy like that away at such a tender age?'

I couldn't hear her husband's reply. My mood darkened as I slide further along the wooden slatted seating into the waiting room for comfort away from the open door and looked around. The cream walls were dotted with posters extolling the fun of train travel that could take you to castles in Scotland, beaches in Devon and cathedrals in Durham and Salisbury.

Steam billowed over the platform and through the open door as my little suburban train heralded the continuation of my journey. She took my hand and lead me to the last carriage, the Guard's van.

'Good luck, little one.' She put a comforting hand on my shoulder as I climbed aboard. I waved back, my eyes fixed on her kind face as we slowly edged away from the station on the way to westwards towards the lowering sun.

I wasn't the only living being on this journey. Opposite me as I sat down, where mounds of cages, all occupied by yellow chicks. My presence seemed to interest them as they became more animated. I brushed my hand along the bars. Their little beaks uncertain whether I was friend or foe. Their future was as uncertain as mine as we sped through the green fields. What lay in store for these little yellow creatures who jostled and flapped at each other. A field where they could roam freely and risk the mouth of a fox or the safety of a cosy warm shed but little liberty. I began to feel stronger about myself for the first time since I left Chester hours earlier. I needed to overcome the fear and trepidation that had permeated my body in the weeks since I realized I was being sent away from the security of my home and my favourite possessions on the shelves in my bedroom.

At my final train stop, I was met on the platform by an elderly man and a taxi in the form of an old Austin A40 that laboured up the hill from Kilgetty Common and through the stone gate posts onto a gravel driveway. My mind slipped back momentarily to some of the impressionable scenes from Charles Dickens novel, Nicholas Nickleby, that my previous teacher read it me and I attempted to join in, getting stuck on difficult words. I half expected to see Dotheboys Hall, not Selwyn House and be confronted by Squeers who beat and starved the boys, pocketing their parents' money. I was relieved, as the little car came to a halt, to see a wide welcoming set of stone steps leading to an impressive set of open doors from which an old man with an impressive grey-white moustache and almost no hair on his golden pate but long wisps tucked behind his generous ears and a smile of welcome that shone from his eyes. It's difficult to read facial expressions, but the eyes are a give-away. My initial impression of him, was kindly but weak, but how that was to impact on me was an unknown. A flash of George Orwell's Animal Farm regime caught me off guard for an irrational moment as I remembered another story from the same junior school-teacher.

'Welcome, Master Simkins. I'm the Headmaster.'

'Thank you, Sir.'

'Matron will show you around. You are one of the early ones. Give to time to settle in.'

I looked across at Matron. Nothing like my mother but she had an air of comfort about her. Ample in stature, kind in demeanour. I took to her immediately and as the Headmaster stood aside, I followed her dutifully through the entrance, along the corridor to the left and up three flights of stairs into a large room. There, in lines of five on each side of a large window, stood ten black metal beds with light blue blankets tucked in at each corner and all the way up to a white starched sheet and crisp white pillow. She took out a card label with my name on it.

'As you're the first, which bed would you like?'

'I can choose?'

I looked around the dormitory and marched over to the window and looked out at the darkening scene stretching over the common, beyond the trees that lined it disappearing towards the dark waters of the sea.

'This one, please, Matron.' I sat on the bed. It was much harder than mine at home. She must have seen my grimace.'

'Better for you, young man. You'll get used to it very quickly. Now put those things in your locker and come with me. When did you last have a meal?' She opened my tin and looked at the paper wrappers and empty bottle. I had been travelling for over five hours.

'A long time ago.' I looked at my watch. 'Four hour and six minutes, except for a glass of milk at Carmarthen.'

She looked at me and I thought she was going to accuse me of impudence. Instead, she took my hand. 'Come on Mr. Precision, let me introduce you to cook.'

Cook, I was to find out over the next few weeks and months, was perhaps a misnomer but on this occasion, she must had excelled herself. The toast wasn't burnt, the fried egg nestling on top looked like one, not a crisp grease-ladened cardboard combination that threatened dislodge your front teeth when she was catering for a full house.

Matron reappeared with an older boy soon after, as I sat there staring at the dining room walls feeling a little lonely, but now the pangs of hunger had been satiated.

'This is Billy Harris. He's been here a few years now. Knows the ropes.'

'I stood up, putting out my hand which I had been taught was the polite thing to do. He ignored it.

'Hi, Billy, nice to meet you.' I was nervous and that's when my Liverpudlian accent came to the fore.

'Remember, you need to call me, Harris.' He tried to imitate the Scouser accent, enunciating the words miserably. 'To fit in here you'll need to talk properly, sonny.'

He clearly thought that as an established boarder, he could demand absolute observance to any orders he might deem necessary, however inconsidered they may be.

I listened to his Welsh accent, trying to practice it silently as he marched around the buildings with me respectfully in tow a few paces behind, into the grounds pointing out this and that. I soon had a picture of what my life was going to be like. Watching him stride over the ground, I was already making judgments about him. I felt a pang of disquiet. I decided to see how matters developed. Stay away, be wary, melt into the background, seemed to be the sensible options for the moment.

I had managed to sleep alone in my dormitory without disturbance from the recurrent nightmare that I usually suffered from and so I began to relax. As other boarders arrived over the next day and the regime of daily life began. Bells rang, alarms awoke you each day, boys scattered here and there, segregated by age but not performance save on the sports field. And there was Billy Harris, top of the pecking order but not of the school, surrounded by his 'yes men'. My initial disquiet about Harris had been right and so far, as I watched him carefully, I managed to avoid any real contact with him in the early days as our paths rarely crossed despite the relative smallness of the confines of our home on the hill.

Although I didn't know it, our lives were destined to entwine over the next year in many ways that both frightened me and gave me great satisfaction, an inner strength that never left me from those days in the early 1950s.

I cannot remember the exact words or who said them, but I took them to be my survival technique until I no longer needed to worry. *Never let anyone see that they have humiliate you. Stand tall despite the pain. Take what's coming and in the end, they'll try to save face, usually by laughing or making some crass observation. Then it will be you who have won. You will have beaten the bully.*

In front of the line of outbuildings that were our classrooms, was a large courtyard where breaktimes saw most younger ones running around, others standing, talking in small groups or lounging against the large trees that bordered an out of bounds area that in Spring saw a carpet of daffodils and bluebells. Standing, as he always did, on the top step leading to the Senior's classroom at the end of the line, was Harris as usual surrounded by his guard of yellow bellies. One came over to where I was standing.

'Harris wants a word.'

'What about?'

'Not for me to say.' He grabbed my arm and pulled me over to the steps. I'd witnessed these events from afar and knew that all eyes were on me as I stood in front of him looking up from the bottom step. Not a word was said. He straightened and stepped down in front of me. His face was within inches of mine, close enough to see his badly scoured teeth, mercury fillings holding most of his lower molars in place. He stepped back a pace and raised his voice, demanding attention from all around.

'I don't like your accent or your attitude.' Then he raised his foot and kicked me. I fell back and straightened, unwilling to capitulate, unlike those I had witnessed on many previous occasions before. He kicked me again and again. He expected submission, tears, forgiveness for my attitude. He got nothing. Each time, after each blow, I straightened and looked at him. I felt real anger but kept it hidden within my bruised body. It wasn't a victory as he hadn't been beaten, yet. He smiled. 'There'll be a next time. Maybe you'll wish you'd apologized.'

Had those watching Harris, the bully, learned anything? I hoped so.

From that moment on, Harris didn't try to imitate my accent. I had now developed an acceptable Welsh lilt to my words and voice, nor did he want another confrontation that would undermine his supremacy amongst equals. Whilst I witnessed others succumb, I was left alone. However, Harris had a festering desire to seek dominance and adulation from his peers and juniors. Bullies always do. He never forgot my resilience, my stubbornness, never to give in to him.

It seemed to me that all the staff were blind to the events that took place daily in breaktimes. Boys can be sadistic and those with the more dominant characters encouraged those weaker ones to seek protection by becoming their "yes men".

Minor misdemeanours, walking on the wrong side of a corridor, talking after lights out, being late, tie not straight, all these you would expect to be dealt with by verbal admonishment from the staff, but in Harris's presence, it was a beating offence. Taken away to some hidden part of the grounds, usually behind the woodshed, and made to confess your sins with the swish of a garden cane. There were always lookouts to ensure anonymity. Harris had the amazing ability of finding weak spots in the boys. I recall one poor soul who inadvertently confessed he hated water. It wasn't long after that, on a trip to the seaside, that he found himself spewing out seawater after being held under by some of Harris's "yes men" for a little too long. His other treatment, reserved for new boys, was his initiation welcome. Head held down the WC pan with the flush drenching the unfortunate boy.

It was a reign of tyranny for a lot of boys. No-one would ever have the fortitude or the strength to report Harris and so the regime kept its tight grip life at school.

I learned very early on never to leave food that I disliked on my plate. Harris and his followers had eyes on every smaller boy's plates. The Food Police pounced on anything not eaten. Donations of the uneaten given next time it was served and in a quiet place away from prying eyes, the offender was forced to clear a full plate. Better than a beating, maybe? One soon found each other's likes and dislikes with surreptitious donation or plate swap, so that the Food Police were denied their fun. However, on one occasion, my best friend was struggling with his bowl of rhubarb and custard. I'd been tardy and not noticed. Quickly I exchanged my empty bowl for his and started to sup my way through it.

Harris was summoned. He looked at me as if I had committed murder. I goaded him with my Liverpudlian accent.

'And what are you proposing, Harris? I like that pudding more than Robinson, so he gave me his.'

'You're a liar. Isn't he Robinson?'

'He likes rhubarb and custard.'

'What's going on here?'

'Cook had arrived and broke up the altercation for the time being. Harris walked away, looking over his shoulder, mouthing, "just you wait and see".

There are still foods that even now, I cannot eat without feeling revulsion as bile rises in my throat.

My fourth term, I was introduced to a new game, rugby, with my contemporaries. No more the round ball that my team Everton played with. New boys had been kept away from the rugby pitch until it was deemed sensible, by whom and when, I never discovered. At first it must have looked ridiculous. We all ran around following the ball, like a shoal of fish. It soon became obvious with a bit of organization the fastest runner could be tackled if we spread out across the field to stop him, only then did passing the ball become a better option. It was beginning to feel like a good game. Soon, a few of us were elevated to play at the next level, Harris' level. I thought nothing of it, after all, it was just a game to win if you could. It wasn't long before I made what turned out to be a grave error of judgment in a practice game of no consequence. Never make Harris look like a fool.

During the early part of the game, I had avoided his tackles, first by a hand-off that sent his face into contortions of rage as he fell backwards into the mud and then by a swerve that left him clasping at an empty space. Towards the end of the game, he tackled me and wrestled me to the ground with the ball. In piled the yes men: I was buried underneath, still clutching the ball. The last thing I saw was a boot coming in from my left. Seconds later, I saw the Headmaster's face looking at me with concern, around him like a halo were the muddied faces of several of my team-mates but the one face I'll never forget was Harris. His smile told me all. It was his boot that had made deliberate contact just behind my bloodied left ear. He'd got his revenge. He'd managed to knock me out.

'He's very lucky not to have anything other than mild concussion, Matron. I assume it was an accidental knee or boot?'

'Yes, Doctor, probably someone being a bit too enthusiastic. Rugby can be a dangerous game. Not for the faint-hearted even at this tender age.'

'Later that afternoon, I was awoken by someone sitting at the end of my bed.

'How are you feeling, Brian,' came the soft voice of Reverend Williams.

'Not too bad, thank you, Sir.'

'I saw your feet under the covers, moving as if you were dancing. Are you sure, you are okay?'

'I saw the concerned look on his face.

'Well, not exactly.' I paused to collect my thoughts. 'I've just had a weird dream, very weird.'

'Want to tell me about it?'

'Promise, Sir, you won't laugh.' He nodded sincerely.

'Well, I was standing on sand, wet sand. If I stood long enough, the water welled over my feet, so I had to keep moving. It was a dark place and I needed to escape. I was frightened. I turned to my left and there was a wall of flame advancing towards me. On my right was a fierce storm with lightning forking through the sky. I turned away from the blinding light and there in front of me were the jaws of a creature wide enough to swallow me. I revolved around to see the raging water with waves so high, they were cresting and crashing down. I was trapped.' I caught my breath, I had been speaking so quickly. 'Then, I looked up and above me was a beautiful blue sky, no clouds in sight. My refuge from this dark frightening place.'

He smiled at me. 'You've taken my Old Testament stories too literally, Brian. Let me tell you what I believe that story means. You know that I said these stories were allegories. Each one has a hidden meaning for those who choose to look into them deeply enough.'

'Sir, who's to say your interpretation is correct.'

'Well, Brian, that's for you to judge. I think you have been reliving the moments that you were remembering before and after being hurt. Your subconscious thoughts were a mixture of your fears. What could have been a much more serious injury, and relief that you were recovering and could live another day. Think about the images?'

He smiled as he saw me relax. 'Now work calls. Just sleep and we'll see you out and about soon.'

'Thank you, Sir.'

As he disappeared through the door, my thoughts returned to the images in the dream. I never told him that wherever I had turned in that subconscious state, I had seen vividly that smile of Harris in the crashing waves, the fork of lightning, the wall of flame and the jaws of that hideous creature.

I turned my head on the pillow closing my eyes, the swelling behind my left ear began to throb.'

There many times during my days recovering under the constant watch of Matron that I wanted to cry out that it was no accident but kept quiet. I'd made up my mind and fate was to take its place in my plans towards the end of that Spring Term.

In early March, the first signs of influenza hit the school and within days sickness spread from one dormitory to another. It can be a deadly virus. Mine started with a sore throat and a runny nose, but I recovered after a few days in bed. As I lay there, I was reminded of my little book of facts and figures. Looking around, I wondered if any of the boys would become one of the half a million worldwide who died each year from the virus. In 1918/9, 50 million died from a particularly virulent strain. My thoughts inevitably returned to Harris and how I was going to extract revenge on him once this was over. He could have killed me that day and he just smiled.

Providence stepped in. Harris's case was severe. My thoughts of revenge hoped that he'd succumb and that his bullying days would therefore end. He was isolated away from the rest of us in sickbay, just across the hallway from where I was lying. Daily bulletins indicated he was likely to be sent to hospital soon. He was still very ill but stable. I saw, on my visits to the bathroom that Matron, when she wasn't attending to us, spent the day in her room adjacent to where Harris was lying, eyes closed, exhausted and sedated. As my ideas coalesced, I became obsessed with the thoughts of extracting justice by bringing this sadistic bully, who had traumatized many smaller boys to an extent that they would probably never forget the misery he caused them in their tender years. I malingered as much as I could exaggerating lethargy and feigning sleep most of the day, but I was making mental notes on the sickbay routine. Harris was the only resident. As Matron slept at night, he was alone. I suppose it was my father's death that created a fascination in the moment of death itself and what actually occurs within the body and the outward and inward signs that pathologists look for in post-mortems. A ghoulish obsession in the mind of an eleven year old. I had not yet recognized that my knowledge may or may not already have been formulated but I read widely of the various methods used by those seeking to end the life of others. Most of the methods of the past were now useless with the emerging systematic approach of the forensic science of detection. I had read that poisons were easily detectable and, in any case, they were not available in our sickbay, so I immediately discarded this method of my revenge on Harris for his bullying and his wreckless attempt to inflict permanent injury on me. Smothering was a possibility, but I was not sure that I had the strength to prevent him from fighting back when he realized what was happening. The human body, even when weakened, has a remarkable sense of danger. Adrenaline would course through his body mustering more strength than I could probably overcome. In addition, it was detectable as it left tell-tail signs such as blood spots in the eyes when no other signs were evident. After much lively debate under cover of darkness lying in my sick bed, I came to believe my method would work and would probably go undetected.

In a school where Harris was nearly the eldest at thirteen, you can imagine that our chemistry department, or rather small classroom, was a simple stepping-stone to secondary school chemistry. All we had was one Bunsen burner, a few pipettes and syringes. Anything that was in any way combustible or corrosive was locked away elsewhere only to be brought out on the day of demonstration. The room contained all that I needed, a 240 millilitre syringe. I knew in which drawer they were kept so whilst the whole school slept, I put on my dressing gown and crept out of the dormitory, down the stairs out of the back door and into the cold air. Ten minutes later with one syringe safely in my pocket I retraced my steps. The appearance of a light being switched on upstairs, caused me to shrink into the shadows of a doorway on the first floor. My heart was thudding in my chest as I took some deep breaths to calm myself. I waited what seemed like an eternity as the minutes passed and the cold began to creep into me. Still, I waited. Eventually I heard the flush of the lavatory. The light was extinguished. I had no idea where the person had come from or how long it would take them to find sleep again, but as I was shivering with cold and decided to risk returning to my bed. I stopped outside the door to my dormitory and listened, turned and opened the bathroom door. I sat on the lavatory and reached up to the high-level cistern. It was cold and damp to the touch as if it hadn't been used recently. Buoyed by my discovery that whoever it had been, it wasn't somebody from my floor, I flushed the WC and got back to bed.

The next day, alone in bed and very tired, I had to figure a way to change the syringe needle as the chemistry version was much too large for what I had in mind. As Matron had administered all of us with injections over the last few weeks, I assumed she would have disposed of the spent needles in some safety box in her office. I needed access. I was going to have to rely on her assumption that we were all innocent little boys who couldn't possibly do any real harm. Next day, feigning a raging headache, I knocked on her door.

'What are you doing here, you need to be back in bed?'

I probably looked the part, a sleepless night, pale and stooped, I explained how I felt. I looked around, she took my arm and felt for my pulse then looked at her watch counting the seconds. She took a key from her desk and opened an adjoining walk-in cupboard. Up, around the desk, hand in the green disposable box and back again, stuffing them into my dressing gown pocket.

'Here.' She handed me an Aspirin and a glass of water. I picked up the glass.

'Show me your hand.'

'Pardon.'

'Your hand. There's blood on it.'

'I looked at the glass and put it down. One of the needles that were hidden in my pocket had punctured a small hole in my palm.

'Where did that come from?'

'I looked horrified and stumbled over what to say.

'Splinter. From the floor in my dorm. Not very steady on my legs at the moment. Took it out earlier, just before I came here.'

'You can never be too careful.' With that she brushed the brown solution of Acriflavin over the small puncture mark. 'It will sting for a while. Don't rub your eyes. Now back to bed with you.'

I slept most of the day, waiting for night to fall and my fellow patients to sleep. Under cover of the blankets with my torch battery rapidly fading, unscrewed the large needle replacing it with one of the new smaller ones. I pulled back the plunger, sucking in air and pressed it down gently feeling the coldness as air brushed my face.

Is you know I have an unhealthy obsession with death. It has been close to me from an early age, so it isn't surprising. Air embolisms block the passage of blood in the system, Divers are prime candidates for this cause of death, hence recompression in a hyperbaric chamber. I became certain that my method of ensuring Harris's departure would go undetected. I hoped that it would be unlikely that any special precautions would be taken during his postmortem examination. I now know that they could have used a spirometer on his heart ventricles and carry out a brain tissue dissection to establish an unusual cause of death, but back then, well, I was an amateur in such matters. What constitutes a lethal dose of air into an artery for humans is unknown. It can vary between 90mls for an old man to 130mls for a healthy victim. I was to inject through Harris's vein not an artery, so more was needed. Satisfied, I hid the redundant needles and looked around the makeshift hospital dormitory. There were only two other occupants still recovering. They were breathing shallowly, deep in sleep.

Slowly, I pulled back my bed covers and stood on the black gloss painted floorboards. I knew which ones groaned under pressure and avoided them. The hallway was empty, no lights anywhere. I gently grasped the sickbay handle and turned it fully and pushed open the door just enough to slide through. In front of me was Harris, breathing quietly. He appeared to be still heavily sedated. His left arm was draped over the blanket, palm upwards.

Two round plasters covered the sites of intravenous injections and blood samples in the crook of his elbow. I put on a pair of the surgical gloves from the adjacent table and carefully removed one of the plasters, intending to reuse it later. I was relieved to see bruising present on his skin around the puncture holes. He had been here so long that some had turned yellow whilst the more recent were still blue.

Everything was falling into place beautifully. I took the syringe from my pocket. No need for sterilization for this one injection. Harris stirred as I took hold of his arm, but his eyes remained closed. Steadying my right hand against the bed covers, I sucked in 250mls of air. I wanted to be sure so I decided that 190mls would be my target. Carefully hovering above the latest injection site, I pushed the needle into the vein. A trace of blood entered the empty syringe. His eyes flickered open and stared at me as I slowly and deliberately depressed the plunger. I smiled at him and whispered, 'Just an accident' as I replaced the old plaster and watched long enough to see him slip into unconsciousness.

'Is this true?'

'I wrote it.'

'I realize that, but did you kill that child?'

'Yes.'

'Why?'

'You've read why. He deserved it. He was a bad piece of work. He didn't just bully me once. He was a constant threat to me. He tried to kill me. There were many others who suffered at his hand and probably still carry the scars.'

'So, let me try to understand. You murdered another boy who bullied you and others. You drew up an elaborate premediated plan, all its details, researched the forensics so that it would appear to be a death from natural causes.

'Yes.'

'How did you feel, watching Harris slip into an irreversible coma?'

'It was strange really, as I lay in bed, I imagined the air being sucked along his venous system towards the right side of his heart. Instead of just his blood entering it would be my air and some of his blood. No way could his lungs now function properly. I could envisage the overload of air being pumped back to the left side of his heart and then through his arterial system to his brain. Harris lapsed into a coma very quickly as I watched. No emotional sympathy passed through my mind, in fact, I was elated at his passing.'

Chapter 15

Mike Apartment

Hillary put down the papers and rubbed her eyes.

'Mike, I've just finished Simkins' confession about killing that boy, Harris, at his prep school.'

'Quite a story, if it's true. We are so naïve these days about life back then.'

'Why would he make it up?'

'Just to massage his own frustration of not being able to do anything about it, in reality, at his age.'

'You mean now he can look back with some psychological relief that he hadn't been such a coward?'

'Yes, something like that.'

'Only one way to find out for sure. You're right, I will take a virtual journey down to West Wales on the computer, as they say, some research. May save a trip.'

'Here, your turn, I've done what I can for the moment.' Hilary stood and left the computer seat for Mike.

'What did you find out about our Dr Carling?'

'She has links with the local Oncology Department of several hospitals, presumably to assist in mentally stabilizing their thoughts and worries about cancer and end of life.'

'Was Simkins referred to her because he has cancer?'

'Maybe.'

'Anyway, does the reason matter? He is talking to her and we're listening in. You do your research, whilst I settle in.'

Mike turned to the computer and smiled at the thought of Hillary moving in permanently.

There certainly was an influenza outbreak in the year Simkins referred to in conversation with Dr Carling. Using MI6's automatic connection with the Registry of Births Deaths and Marriages, Mike started searching for William Harris, the year and approximate date and the location. A common name in West Wales came up with two hits. He only printed one of the two death certificates, the one that referred to the cause of death as "influenza". He shouted to Hilary. No answer. He walked into the spare room. Hilary was half dressed lying asleep on the bed. He sat beside her and kissed her hair. She stirred and smiled at him.

'Catching up on the early start from Moscow. Sorry.'

'Billy, William Harris died from the flu. Same school is reported on the Certificate as place of death. Right timing. Supports Simkins version in all but cause of death.'

Hillary sat up immediately. 'Interesting. Saves us a long journey to West Wales.' As she settled into the pillows against the headboard. Mike snuggled beside her, but by now she was wide awake.

'You can leave that for later, Mr Randell, then continued, 'so far we have Albert's allegations that Simkins was responsible for Penfold's incineration, Parson's missing body and Albert's obsession that Simkins somehow got him dismissed, and now Simkins's own confession of killing Harris.'

'Seems to be a pattern here,' Mike concluded. At that moment Mike's computer registered a new attachment from Albert with the words 'Here's another Session. We're dealing with a serial killer, Mike.'

'Maybe, but there's a huge time gap between events.'

Hillary was silent as she put pen to paper, marking out the timeline. The Bully was the first, then Parsons followed recently by Penfold.

'There is only one explanation, Mike. Work took over, building from employee to partner takes time and long hours.'

'Could be until someone crosses his path that triggers his pathological behaviour, or we are wasting our time on Walter James Mitty alias Brian Simkins character.'

'I remember reading that James Thurber novel some time ago. Mild man, meek with a vivid imagination.'

'I mentioned Mitty because the more I think of what we know to date, the MOs, if you can call them that, are in the realms of….'

'Fantasy?' interrupted Hillary.

'Yes. Thurber's book had a darker side amongst the humour. When we analysed the book at school, I think the conclusion was that Mitty was well-meaning but when strangers robbed him of some of his dignity, he became a different person.'

'The devil may care killer,' laughed Hillary.

'That is exactly it,' said Mike with a concerned look on his face. 'One of his fantasies.'

Chapter 16

The Headmaster

Session 5

After Harris's death, my life took on a much better aspect. I had already made some close friends and started to concentrate on my schoolwork. The underlying all-embracing fear evaporated. I felt free. I looked forward to returning to school after the holidays for the first time. Home became less important. It was there, safe but boring. My only friends were far away. We were just beginning to hear the exciting new music, rock and roll. It was the late 1950s

However, over two of those holidays, tragedy befell our family again. My mother's father, my grandfather died when I was home at half-term. I'd known him as a figure of mild but Victorian authority. I only remember him as he was then, he spent days, months and years languishing in bed, every day propped up by numerous pillows with a mountain of papers scattered around him with pencil in hand. I used to sit with him, transfixed as columns of figures were transformed into totals as his pencil swept over the paper.

'How do you do that so quickly?' I'd ask. 'I know my additions, but you are super-fast.'

'Practice, many years of practice.'

He'd been and still was, an accountant for a firm of haberdashers and was also a share holder in the company. I learned that years later.

'Can I help?'

He passed me a column of figures expressed, before decimalization, in pounds, shillings and pence. (Twelve pence to the shilling and twenty shillings to the pound). He then explained how he did it. Not necessarily in order in the column.

'If you see an easy addition, like this 45 then two places away a 15, add them, 60 then go back to the 8 and so on. Interestingly, I still use that method now even when I'm using a calculator.'

Over the next few weeks, we tested each other's speed. Although I got quicker, I confess he always won, sometimes by a whisker but I knew he had slowed down to encourage me. He never wanted my efforts to go unpraised. He knew I thrived on encouragement, never criticism. Sometimes when he had finished, he would test me on multiplication and division. I loved those times but was always aware that I should not interfere too much as he was working, earning a living.

One morning, I went to give him his morning cup of tea. He was propped up in bed as usual, but something was different. His mouth was wide open, a slither of saliva had dried on his blue lips, his eyes were closed and he was very pale. His hands were cold on mine, and he didn't stir when

I touched him. I stood back momentarily and stared at him. So, this is what a silent permanent sleep looks like. Yesterday, he smiled at me and spoke to me. Now he can't do either. Was his last moment of consciousness, peace or pain? I would never know until it was my inevitable turn. I rushed out of the room.

'Grandma, I think Grandad's dead,' I shouted.

I remember the hushed silence. The usual warm kindness vanishing instantaneously as she rushed out of the kitchen with my mother in tow. Moments later, I heard the telephone click.

I never saw him again, I was banished, except not entirely. From my vantage point on the stairs, I watched the Doctor arrive with his black bag and disappear into Grandad's room. An hour later the Undertakers removed him under a white sheet on their trolley through the front door. Curtains twitched across the way as I ran into the front to watch him being pushed into the recesses of the black van, and the doors being closed. That was finality for me.

The curtains in the front of our house were pulled across the windows. Darkness fell on Holly Bank and on me. Only later did I understand why he was bed-ridden. During WW1, his regiment was subjected to a gas attack at Ypres in Northern France. His lungs were permanently damaged, and he was invalided out of army. I look back at that short period with just him and me together with happiness then sadness that he was no longer around. Maybe, he was the father I never had the chance to talk to, to learn from, but he was taken away and with that, a soft touch and loving bond.

It was only a few weeks later, after his funeral that I wasn't allowed to attend, that I answered the front doorbell. It had been a vicious day of rain then early evening November fog. There stood two police officers, water dripping from their capes.

'Hello,' said the taller of the two, as I gazed at them.

'Come in,' I said politely.

They followed me from the porch into the hall as my mother and grandmother came to see what was happening. I was relegated to standing aside at the back of the hall. A whispered conversation ensued, and they disappeared into the sitting room and closed the door. My curiosity was too great as I bent down and put my ear to the keyhole.

'There's been an accident.'

**

To me those words were a wholly bad beginning to a conversation. On my last trip by bus to Chester, I had seen the aftermath of an accident. As I peered out of the window of the bus, as it slowed almost to a stop, I saw an inert figure of a man lying in the road, a few feet from my face. I remembered the blood that had seeped from a cut on his head as it lay pooling on the tarmac. I was transfixed and couldn't look away.

'There's been an accident. You shouldn't be looking,' said my mother realizing what had happened.

Those words had the opposite effect. My eyes became glued to the wet road outside and the uncovered body that lay on it. It must have happened moments earlier. I tried to come up with an explanation and then I saw the motorcycle lying in the hedge and just behind, over my shoulder a small lake of water standing in the road. My attention turned back to him. All I could see was his brown hair slicked across his face from the pouring rain and red seeping from his forehead. My mother's hands turned my head away from the window that was misting under my breath.

**

After the police had left, an air of pure sadness descended on Holly Bank, yet again, but far worse than Grandad's passing. My mother had lost her little brother, my Grandmother, her only son and Teddy's wife, her husband and their three very young children, their father. I picked up short pieces of the conversation trying to put together a picture of what had happened. Apparently, Teddy had been given a lift home and there had been a head-on collision in the fog.

Why had there been a head-on collision? Who had been on the wrong side of the road? How had he died? I knew it had been foggy, maybe one or both drivers had become disorientated. The impact would have been devastating even at a combined speed of 60 mph. Teddy, relaxing as passenger tend to, would have been catapulted towards the dashboard and the screen. The velocity of the impact would have been far greater than would have been survivable as his brain smashed against the front of his skull. In its traumatic state, normal messaging would have been impossible, and his heart and other organs would shut down, causing immediate death.

I felt really sorry for my cousins even though I didn't know them well. They had lost their father, never to play with him again. It struck a chord with me. I knew the devastation it would cause, hidden inside each one of them, never to be forgotten.

**

'You had a bad time. I'm sorry.'

'It was unnerving.'

'What do you mean by "unnerving"?'

'Well, I suppose that I had recovered from the early days of being away from home and was beginning to enjoy life in West Wales and then, in the blink of an eye, home became somewhere again where bad things happened. I was unnerved.'

I had a developing fascination in the way the human body shuts itself down after years of maintaining life, morbid, maybe. Interesting certainly, but for me, something I needed to understand. After all, it seemed to me that I had been surrounded by it.

Any organ in the body can fail first, then another and so on, but apart from Harris's death where his brain died first, the human body dies from a failure of ventilation or circulation. Some of us stop breathing first, after which the heart will beat for a minute or two before everything begins to fail or, in others, the circulation stops through low blood pressure and the heart stops for lack of oxygen. Grandad just faded away, his blood pressure fell slowly as he was sleeping, and his breathing became shallower until there was no oxygen to sustain his body. My subsequent research had given me comfort and I was relieved that they would have felt no pain. I had assumed that was how my father died when they slowly turned off the lung machine. My Grandfather had already suffered enough serving King and country in 1917. He had always considered that he was the lucky one, thousands lay in the mud, never to return from Northern France. He never talked about the slaughter that he and other conscripts or volunteers saw as they entered a world none of them could have imagined. Shell shocked and desperate, many could not face another day in the trenches and refused to fight. Disaffection in the ranks was not allowed to spread as the cowards were court-marshalled within days and shot. Many were just teenage boys. Only with hindsight were these barbarities recognized for what they were, the then unrecognized medical condition of Post-Traumatic Stress Disorder.

**

'So, you moved to a new school.'

'How old were you?'

'Twelve.'

'Wasn't the usual entry age thirteen for Common Entrance?'

'It is, but I cheated!'

'Cheated? In the exam?'

'Well, not exactly. I was very good at some subjects as you may have gathered.'

'So why cheat?'

'Well, there were a few compulsory subjects, one's I really wasn't interested in, where I was mediocre, languages.'

'What happened. Do you want to tell me?'

'I received some unspoken help through French and Latin.'

'How, from whom?'

'Reverend Williams was the invigilator. Every now and again he'd walk around then look over my shoulder. He and I got on well, there was a kind of invisible link. I think he felt sorry for me, only child, witnessing death personally on two occasions, trying to come to terms with the fragility of life, but it was never mentioned. He had an amazingly optimistic outlook. He had his faith. I was christened into the faith of the Church of England, but nothing had clicked for me, it just did not seem relevant. He knew that I respected him and also what I was capable of, so on two occasions, at least that is what I remember, I had written an incorrect answer. He knew that I would look around as he hovered, so he shook his head. He would stay until I corrected it and then move on without a word.'

'Did you feel it was wrong?'

'No. He did the right thing and that is what I assume he felt about it.'

'I see.'

I had hoped that the sadistic elements of my early school life were not going to play a decisive part in the next one. And whilst corporal punishment had its part to play, it was in a much more governed manner. Transgressions had to be serious, smoking, fighting or stealing.

'You've skipped a few years here, I notice?'

'Yes, those years were growing up, maturing if you like, nothing exceptional worth noting.'

'Really?'

'Well, if I am truthful only one matter, actually. If you read on, it's all there.'

'As a new boy, I had little contact with the Headmaster. He was there for the older boys, but my only contact was in Latin classes. There was always a mutual dislike, unsaid loathing is too harsh a description, but I knew to keep my distance. He was a squat man with receding hair. He hid his eyes behind metal rimmed glasses. They were small and penetrating, harsh, uninviting and unsmiling. Even at my age, I looked down on him when standing. His bearing was naturally aggressive but controlled. His smile, when it did filter through, bore a feeling of distrust. The other nauseating fact about him was his absolute devotion to his dog, Gurt, some pedigree version of a large smooth haired agile hunter that accompanied him on long walks alone across barren marsh and moorland adjacent to the school, but out-of-bounds to us.

'I'm still unsure of why he decided from an early age that I was trouble because we rarely crossed paths and I certainly tried to avoid him. I decided that he had great prejudices, chips on his shoulders, if you like. These preconceived, unfavourable evaluations of me were designed to overpower my own beliefs and values, to force compliance into the existing system and to subdue personal characteristics. They manifested themselves in pathetic unjust ways and festered in my mind too. He had his favourites, although I am sure some of them just put up with him for what he was. His true pets were solid and boring who would not and could not challenge him. It may sound arrogant, but they were the sort who you'd try to avoid sitting next to in case your thoughts turned to suicide as you tried to blot out their droning voices and hoping they would lapse into silence sooner rather than later.'

'You really didn't like him, did you? Were you afraid of him?'

'I suppose so, especially at the beginning but then I began to realise slowly that there was nothing he could do to influence change within me. I think he saw that as the years progressed, but he still tried.'

The first real challenge came when I decided that our Combined Cadet Force was not an organization that I wanted to have anything to do with, even though it was a compulsory institution that all boys had to take part in. My grandfather had given his life up in 1917, my father had come back from Africa in 1944 too ill with amoebic dysentery to fight again, so I grew up hating war and anything to do with its perpetuation. Cleaning boots until they shone like mirrors, buffing brass buckles to reflect the light, pressing khaki trousers with a damp hot iron until the creases were pristine on both sides, marching up and down like clockwork soldiers, all seemed such a waste of precious time to me.

I had no choice as my kit was allocated. My protestations against this regime went unheeded so I took matters into my own hands, brass buckles didn't shine, trouser creases appeared in the wrong places, boots didn't seem to have been cleaned properly. Week after week, I spent hours being detained, doing what I hated. The only part of those dreadful months that I enjoyed was shooting in the miniature range and I may say with some success. However, this part did not overcome my desire to say goodbye to the CCF although I still had juvenile ambitions to represent the school at shooting. The Headmaster was adamant that I should knuckle under and improve my behaviour or say goodbye to shooting. I had to find a way to persuade him. I shot an almost perfect score that found its way to his ear, but still he insisted that shooting and membership of the CCF were a partnership, not one without the other.

In his study, overlooking the arable fields of corn and wheat waving in the breeze in the distance, I stood. Hands behind my back. He looked up, I stared back. Gurt's eyes opened, and the dog gave me a snarl baring his upper teeth. I was not sure whom of the two, I was at this point, fearing most, probably the dog. He opened the conversation.

'Well, what have you got to say for yourself?'

'About what?' I stared back.

'You know perfectly well.'

'Oh, the miniature range.'

'Yes, the miniature range.'

'It wasn't my fault.'.........'Sir.' I added that reluctantly.

'Then who's fault was it?'

'I don't know.'

'You shot out two lamps at your target end,' he seethed, baring his own teeth this time.

'No, Sir.'

'Don't lie to me.'

'Sir, the sights were altered, and the bullets went high.'

'Do you think I'm a fool?' I wanted desperately to say "yes" but held my tongue. He opened a file and his finger darted across the entries. 'Your performance in the Army Corp is abysmal. Your attitude is deplorable. You are letting the side down. Do you know that? What do think would have happened in 1939 if your attitude had prevailed?' He waited for capitulation. I took the plunge.

'I think the concept of the CCF is archaic and does nothing to educate us about our responsibility. There is never going to be another war involving the general population. Hiroshima and Nagasaki taught me that. The Soviet Union can match the West, so everyone knows it is a stalemate. We are all fed up with the slaughter. I'm a pacifist and proud to believe that war solves nothing.'

I could see rage lighting his eyes but there was something holding his wrath at bay. Had I struck a nerve somewhere inside him? That is interesting, I thought in the silence that followed my outburst.

'You're gated for the rest of term and further your dishonourably discharged from the CCF which will be noted when you eventually leave this school. Now get out of my sight.'

I managed to hold my delight in check until I was well clear of his study, then I skipped up the stairs to the library as if I won an enormous sum on the football pools. My euphoria lasted a few days until his retribution started to manifest itself.

First, my appearance on the sports field were curtailed by trumped up charges that saw me sitting for hours in the classroom on my own. These hours were not wasted, I turned them into learning sessions. My position as a Prefect was withdrawn and with that my own study was cleared overnight and I was bungled back from being a privileged citizen to an ordinary one in this repressive regime. The library became my sanctuary, a haven for research. I was not alone, of course not. There were others who had fallen foul of some ideological premise of the Headmaster.

'You've pissed off the old fart, good and proper.'

'Not really, we just didn't see eye to eye over my views on the CCF.' I tried to make light of the situation and my worsening resentment for the old fart.

'Why don't you tell him you're determined to apply to Oxford University and that's why you are spending so much time here in the library. He'd love that.'

'You serious?'

'I did and he's all over me.'

I doubted that, but I did not want to disillusion him. Once he had been crossed, that was it.

'Funny you should say that because I did mention it to Gregory. He said he would put in a word as an old alumnus.'

'I know. Read Divinity and managed a boxing blue at the same time, but it's the old fart you want to speak to direct.'

'I've already asked Gregory to pave the way. These vicars have a mystical manner about them, and he knows me well enough.'

The plan began to work. I was allowed back onto the sports field, my prefectorial status was restored, and the old fart recognized that my academic results were soaring in numbers. I was feeling well with the world until, one evening, I was watching the last tennis match of the day and with Gurt on the lead, the Headmaster approached. He sat beside me on the grass.

'Good evening, Headmaster.'

He turned to me. His grin bearing into me like an executioner delighting in his task.

'Just wanted to say, I cannot and will not recommend your application to my old university. You'll have to apply somewhere else less prestigious.'

I looked at him too stunned to say anything, floored by his metaphorical left hook that knocked my brain out of sync. Finally, I managed one word.

'What?"

'You heard me quite plainly!"

He got up and walked off without a backward glance. He thought he had finally won. My distain, at that moment, turned to hatred for him. It festered below the surface throughout the summer holidays and into the last year of school. I kept my thoughts to myself and my dealings with him on a cautious acceptance level so as to raise no suspicions of my actual state of mind. This man was not going to ruin my life because of some innate hatred of himself that he was unable to admit to or refused to accept. I would find a way to bring justice to bear.

He had never admitted that, under all the outward impression of intellect, power and control over others, he was a coward. On my own admission that I was a pacifist a year or so ago to his face, he had understood and identified with that stance and, I thought that he had been unable to shake his own shame from his mind.

I had recognized this at the time and started to investigate his wartime exploits, searching his military records. I had drawn a blank. He was of military service age. Where had he hidden? What contribution had he made? I found nothing until one day I received a reply from the Salvation Army. Those that did not volunteer were called up and while many of them were not dancing in the streets with joy, they recognised their duty to the country and went to do their bit. So far as the Headmaster was concerned, he had heeded Churchill's warnings of Hitler's global ambitions and opted well before restrictions were imposed to flee by taking a ferry to Ireland and a post teaching in Dublin, gambling on Ireland remaining neutral.

This knowledge of his double standards exacerbated my malign feelings towards him. I watched his daily routine very closely, it varied very little, so I put my plan in place. As the light was fading slowly in late October, I watched as he released the dog from its lead. It bounded across the field towards the reservoir. It had been raining heavily for several days but this evening it was a clear with an ink black luminescent sky above. The dog's nose was hugging the ground, the animal was darting this way and that, then it stopped, lingering on a new intoxicating smell, that of raw meat that I had taken from the kitchen refuse the previous day and tossed it as far as I could towards the forbidden territory around the reservoir where the liquefied soil had lost its strength. Onwards the dog bounded, giant strides, bouncing through the air until it was too late. Its feet became engulfed by the mud as it struggled, digging deeper into the mire.

I watched through my binoculars as the wretched animal's legs began to slowly disappear. The Headmaster's reaction was predictable. He followed him racing towards his destiny as he cast aside the wire fence, driven onwards to save his love. Legs lifted higher and higher as he desperately tried to keep moving forwards, sinking deeper, arms flailing and trashing, as he was swallowed and dragged downwards, finally his head disappearing below the surface. I watched and so did Gurt.

How long can a man survive without oxygen? I looked at my watch, the seconds ticked by. One minute, I looked up and focused the binoculars. Two minutes. No air in his lungs just some acrid water that he's inhaled. Three minutes, his brain cells were shutting down, the seconds ticked on. Only now did I run from my vantage point, shouting the alarm, bursting into the forbidden sanctuary of the Masters' Common Room. All faces turned towards me as I told them what I had witnessed. Four minutes ticked by, little chance of survival. Running across the field, ropes in hand, wooden planks and netting, five minutes. I pointed towards the darkened surface where he had taken his last step. Boards were lowered. Netting unfurled, rope in hand, Mr Bannerman, the athletics teacher, the fittest and strongest amongst the masters, tied one end of the rope arounds his waist and crawled forward, another rope in hand. His broad shoulders stooped forwards as his arms disappeared below the surface into the lake of water and mud, unfurling the rope as he tried to loop it around the Headmaster's chest, fumbling, stretching, pulling, until he was certain it would hold. Six minutes. My job done, I watched as the shout "heave" echoed into the night.

The Headmaster's body slowly rose from the ground, lifeless, heavy with grass and mud, dripping with water as it was dragged closer and closer to firm ground. I watched as his head was tilted to one side. Chest pumped, then air being pushed into his lungs. There was an eerie gurgling sound, water sprang from his mouth. I watched in horror. How could I have got this wrong? But no, nothing more. The silence was interrupted by a whimper as Gurt came and lay beside his master, licking the debris from his face.

That night, as I lay in my bed, a quiet serenity passed through me as sleep came easily. Justice against this tyrant had been long coming and had finally cast him aside. I had to give evidence at the Coroner's Court. My conduct that night was praised for the immediate realisation that time was crucial in the situation I had witnessed. The Coroner had heard evidence from the post-mortem examination that death had occurred moments before he had been dragged out of the swamp. It would have been impossible for any rescue attempt to have been any quicker. I had done my best and so had everyone else. The verdict was Misadventure.

Chapter 17

Present Day - Mike's Apartment

Both Mike and Hilary read a copy each in silence and by the time they had finished, the lowering sun cascaded through the windows beckoning them to take a break.

'Victim number four?'

'It certainly looks like it. Feels the same kind of bizarre MO that he'd would use.'

'What?'

'I've got something nagging at the back of my mind. We need a break. Come on let's get out of here, but one thing first.' Mike typed in Paul Mitchell's private email at the London School of Economics where his old school mate was Professor of Middle Eastern studies. 'Should get a reply that will help. Paul's a font of knowledge. Should save us a lot of unnecessary searching.'

'Where shall we go?'

'You tired?'

'Why?'

'I have this crazy idea.'

Three hours later, just as the station clock struck 8.30 pm, they sauntered, arm in arm, out of the Gare du Nord into the light warm breeze of the Parisienne evening for the short walk to their hotel, feeling refreshed after a couple of hours rest.

'Not such a crazy idea, Mike.'

'Good, we'll forget about the Simkins affair until we get back, agreed?'

Hillary tightened her grip on Mike's arm as they trundled their overnight cases along the cobbled street towards the Mademoiselle Hotel passing between the canal St Martin, the opera House and Sacré Coeur. After checking in, their first port of call was Patio for a drink and to share a simple charcuterie of meat with warm bread and oil together wine, a bottle of rustic red Cabernet Sauvignon. They then strolled along the canal towpath with locals slowly passing the end of the day before retiring to their room.

Despite Mike's assurance that the Simkins investigation would be on hold, he could resist turning on his laptop as they fell back together into the feather pillows against the headboard.

There staring them in the face was Paul Mitchell's reply.

'Hi stranger. Good to hear from you. Interesting request. Did some digging for you. Won't ask why, you'd never tell me anyway. Yes, there was a former pupil, Brian Simkins. Yes, the Headmaster died as you describe. Both, at the school at the same time. The verdict was misadventure. Chasing his dog and drowning in a futile attempt to save the creature. Nothing else. Call me sometime, Mike. Best wishes, Paul. P S

The revised book on Eldridge is due out next month, I'll send you a copy. Your information on the affair was very illuminating.'

'I am never going to sleep now, Mike.'

'Bad idea, hey?'

'Simkins seems to be a very clever one. Nothing sticks.'

'Unless it's a pack of wishful thinking by a man with doubtful courage and there's nothing to stick.'

'Smoke without fire. To my mind it is all too co-incidental,' said Mike turning off the laptop.

Hillary snuggled into him, resting her head on his chest, as he stroked her hair gently. Despite the jumble of thoughts going through her head, she closed her eyes and fell into a deep sleep.

The countryside outside Paris flashed by as Mike closed his eyes momentarily lost in the memories a lazy love making, wandering the back streets hand in hand, breakfast in bed on Saturday morning, coffee and croissants gazing at Sacré Coeur, suddenly he was jolted back to the present as his laptop sprung into life, a message from Albert. He turned the screen so both he and Hilary could read, the latest intrusion into Brian Simkins private life.

Chapter 18

Post-Traumatic Stress Disorder

Session 6

Dr Carling stared across the room. Simkins braced himself mentally for what was to come.

'It seems to me that you react very differently from most of us. Most of us when faced with such a situation as you have just described, concerning the Headmaster, would lock those feelings of loathing and unjustness aside. Just part of life's experience, but you emerge from those situations with dark feelings and have to confront them head-on. You appear to be unable to just ignore them. The question is "Why can't you deal with them in the same way as a normal person?". Does that seem a fair assessment of the situation?

'I'm not sure it does. You're already telling me that I am abnormal.'

'Simply put, your behaviour is abnormal, Brian. Surely you see that?'

'To me there is a need to feel that there has to be justice in a normal society, however small that micro-society is. I told you that my memories extend beyond the norm, into pre and immediate post-natal experiences. Maybe if you don't have these trauma memories of being a prisoner inside your host and the fear of being trapped. You, Barbara, as with the majority of others alive today, are already pre-destined to have those memories overridden by the growth of new nerve cells. Those recollections disappear forever.

'Those nerve cells in my head are still alive with memories. Yours died in those first three years or so. This is a phenomenon that I have been living with for the whole of my life. It won't let go and I cannot hide from it. Heaven knows I have tried.'

'I understand that. However, as I have said before, you have confronted me with a theory that is scientifically unproven, but since our last meeting I have spoken to some of my colleagues concerning your experiences.'

'Can I assume that these were hypothetical conversations?'

'Of course. No names.'

'With what results?

'To be truthful, I have been working on a theory.'

'The same one?'

'No. Hear me out. I just wanted to see if there were any of my colleagues who had experienced a case like the one that you've presented.'

'And? Has anyone?"

'Dr Andrew Pike. He worked in the battle zone in Iraq in the early years between 2004 and 2006. An American soldier had suffered some serious injuries, none were life-threatening, but he was clearly traumatised by what he witnessed. Dr Pike was asked to bring him out of his catatonic state. The soldier internalised everything he had witnessed. He became imprisoned by the events, just as you seem to be telling me.'

'Where's this going. I sometimes think of myself as a prisoner of my past, but again aren't we all?'

'Maybe, but please bear with me for a moment. After his physical injuries healed, Dr Pike continued with the therapy sessions twice a week. That soldier started to talk about his early life, recalling events just as you have. Surprised and sceptical, the sessions continued until Dr Pike came to the conclusion that not only had this soldier developed Post Traumatic Stress Disorder from what he'd seen in Iraq, but he suffered the same experience just after birth.'

'So, this Dr Pike thinks that I suffered undiagnosed PTSD as a baby?'

'I'm not sure, but that was his informed conclusion. He went further by saying that the natural loss of those early neurons is essential and that is why all of us have them replaced as we grow to prevent such a Disorder.'

'Sounds like a research programme waiting for funding.'

'Do you mind if I take you through some tests?'

'Tests? I will be long gone before you finish, dead from this thing inside me that's slowly, inexorably, sapping the life out of me. It's Okay. I get depressed with the thought of dying alone, everything within me unresolved. I have to remind myself that I'm here because of that. So, let's do the tests.

'Oh, by the way, Brian, Dr Pike asked to be consulted as we progress. It was he who sent the questionnaire. I assume you have no objection.'

'None at all as long as confidentiality and anonymity remain paramount and that he has no access to my diaries or their detailed contents.'

'Of course. The tests are only about your early life, the memories from those days. We are having to rely on your objectivity. It's bound to be somewhat unscientific given the circumstances, but your diaries are helpful in that they not only give details of events, but you have added comprehensive notes on your feeling and reactions to those feelings.'

'I therefore assume that I have already answered some of them inadvertently?'

'You're right. I have been through all the questions and from the diaries I have ticked some of the boxes, but I still need clarification on others.'

'Do I get to hear the questions that I have already answered?'

'I do not think that is necessary. Shall we start?'

'Okay, I'm ready.'

'Do you feel sometimes that you are reliving those early events?'

'My immediate answer is "yes", but reliving is a difficult one to assimilate. For example, if I envisage the deaths of Harris and the Headmaster, I think the triggers for each were the distress I was feeling. I got to the point that I had to do something to relieve the pressure. It had become too great to endure any longer. Reminding me of the pain of being dragged into life. It felt like it was happening all again, albeit in a very different form, and I have to make it go away, so I do.'

'Which of these, the reliving or the two solutions, come to you when you dream?'

'Dream? It's a very long time since I recall dreaming. Maybe now I am too tired to dream but you're asking me to go back decades.'

'Yes, I am but surely you have some memories of those dreams?'

'There is one that I cannot forget. I am running away across a ploughed field. The earth is piled up very high, I struggle up and over each furrow onwards towards the safety of the sea and the beach far away, but I never seem make any progress towards the beach. Safety just seems to get beyond my reach. I never knew what happened next as I used to wake up covered in perspiration entangled in the bedsheets.'

'Did you ever resolve the question, what were you running away from?'

'Not for a long time. I used to lie awake trying to figure out why I could only focus on the water and the beach in the distance. I never looked back to see what I was running away from.'

'You're about to tell me something?'

'Am I, how do know?'

'Are you?'

'Yes. I had my first car and one day I decided to drive to where I was born. Now, looking back, it seemed like a strange decision. Not the sort of thing one would think of doing in your early twenties. I drove alone to the Nursing Home where I was born. Strangely, I recognised it as soon as I drove in through the gates. It was still the same building but had been converted into a residential block of apartments. I walked into the gardens. At the back was a wire fence. Beyond I could hear the sea as waves crashed into the beach. It was as if the years had stood still. I peered through. There was no ploughed field. There never had been. In front of me was a stretch of undulating tidal grass and mud.'

'You realised then that the dreams had their roots in reality?'

'Absolutely. I then turned and looked back at the building and realised for the first time that I had been running away from the white coats and blue uniforms that gave me my first breath.'

'Did that dream stop?'

'No. I had hoped it would. I expected it, but it didn't.'

'When did the dream stop?'

'I can't tell you exactly, sometime in my late twenties, I think. They began to get less vivid and fade little by little, no longer waking, sweating, longer periods of time between them. I felt I was shutting them away, saying goodbye. I'll probably have one tonight.

Dr Carling ticked a box on the questionnaire then lifted her head.

'I'm sure you won't. Tell me about "distress" that you mentioned earlier. You said it was a trigger.'

'You're making me feel really fucked up which I'm sure I'm not.'

'Sorry I didn't intend to make a judgement. Instead, I really want to understand how intense that feeling of distress becomes. Is it visual? Can I see it? Tangible or emotional, or maybe a combination?'

'Wow, that's a difficult one. Give me a minute or two.'

'I'm not sure of the relevance but you've prompted me to think of a time of sadness during the time that you wanted me to concentrate on. The two males that left my life, father and grandfather in fairly quick succession, at least it felt like that looking back. Both triggered an unpleasant feeling of being alone, unable to cope. Of course, I did, there was no other choice. This is the distress you are talking about.'

'Yes, the psychological type. Did it intrude into with your daily routine?'

'Routine? Not that I can recall, but there must have been times when I felt sadness, an anxiety but only when my mind was unoccupied and probably at night. That recurring dream became more frequent as I remember. It's strange, now with the cancer diagnosis, I can relate back more succinctly, with more precision.'

'But surely the stresses have increased recently?'

'Certainly, but surprisingly they have had the opposed effect than the one I had expected.'

'What do you mean?'

'Now I can communicate much more freely whereas when I was little, the negative stresses affected greatly my ability to communicate. I had internalised them despite my mind running wild with thoughts and emotions creating vivid anxious moments. Now with the diagnosis, I feel an unusual sense of freedom.'

'So, feeling chronic stress now is something you just push to one side as never before?'

'I think that's right, but there may be another explanation.'

'Which is?'

'Sitting here with my whole life hanging out to dry.'

'I am only referring to your diaries to the age of what, eighteen, as we are trying to concentrate on the very early part of your life for this PTSD experiment. For the moment, we have to forget about the other diaries. Let's digress. When you describe the events leading up to the deaths of Harris and the Headmaster, they seem very coordinated, planned with precision and premeditated. Is there ever a time when the stress is very short term?'

'The stress builds up slowly over time culminating in my making a decision. What I have noticed is that when it reaches a peak, my heart beats faster and great anger creeps into me. At the time of their deaths there is a feeling of exhilaration that causes me to take some deep breaths to calm me down.'

'So, Brian, what you're telling me is those overwhelming feelings can be physical as well, albeit, very short term. Are you ever, in those situations, aware of other images, ones that come from a time past?

'Not images as such, just pictures I've created for myself that represent what I have endured. A bit of a jumble, they change regularly. There was no fixed one that emerges, except that awful dream. That was a constant back then.

Chapter 19

Present Day - Eurostar Journey to London

'Interesting situation developing here, don't you think, Mike?'

'When I was in Belize in the conflict with Honduras, we had a couple of young guys who were flown home to the UK possibly suffering from the Disorder. What I learnt was that in most cases, the symptoms develop during the first month after a traumatic event. In this case a land mine blew up the open top Land Rover that they were following in convoy. Poor buggers were covered in blood and body parts. However, in a minority of cases, there may be a delay of months or even years before symptoms start to appear.

'When I eventually got back to the UK, I became interested in the subject for a while. Apparently, studies show that some people with PTSD experience long periods when their symptoms are less noticeable, followed by periods where they get worse. Other people have constant severe symptoms.

'So, what the experts are saying is that the specific symptoms of PTSD can vary widely between individuals.'

'If I remember correctly, Hillary, they fall into three main categories. The obvious first one involves flashbacks, nightmares. repetitive and distressing images or sensations and physical sensations, such as pain, sweating, feeling sick or trembling.'

'You mean like those from World War One suffering from shell shock.'

'Exactly. No-one then understood the phenomenon. Some poor buggers were shot for cowardice.'

The coffee trolley stopped next to them, and Mike bought two flat whites and a power bar each. He then looked out at the passing countryside, thoughts of those frightening times when he had feared for his own life; bumping along the dusty road into the hills outside Luxor bound and gagged only last year. Then diving out of the plane on his first parachute training drop.

'Mike, you still with me?'

'Sorry, just remembering.'

'Luxor, one of those memories?'

'Yes. I do not suppose they can be forgotten. They just fade with time, but real PTSD sufferers cannot sometimes overcome constant negative thoughts, particularly when there is absolutely nothing they could control about their situation.'

'Like Simkins, reliving pre and post-natal memories.'

'Yes. What were your first memories?'

'One was sitting on my hobby horse that my grandparent had bought for my third birthday and nearly falling off.'

'Anything earlier?'

'No. You?'

'Same age.'

'What are the other categories that you mentioned?' asked Hillary.

'The general heading is avoidance and emotional numbing. This involves avoiding certain people or places that remind you of the trauma or avoiding talking to anyone about your experience.'

'Well, Simkins has left it a very long time.'

'Maybe, but I think he is aware that he's been different for years and tried to work things out himself. He appears to have tried to rid himself of that recurring dream, for example, by revisiting the nursing home where he was born.'

'In the end, he is seeking some sort of closure with these sessions with Dr Carling.'

'I think he finally realised that his attempt to deal with his feelings by trying not to feel anything at all, emotional numbing, hadn't worked. He also wants to understand why he acts the way he does in certain circumstances.'

'Mike, you mean when he feels he is threatened. We have seen he doesn't react like most of us, by turning the other cheek or trying to calm himself."

'Hillary, that's the point, the third category may explain. Given what we have read about

Simkins to date. I think he looks at life as if he's constantly feeling on edge.'

'Hyperarousal, I think is the word,' interrupted Hillary.

'Yes,' said Mike smiling at Hillary.

'That's where his angry outbursts have led him to seek an alternative remedy. One that does not fit our view the world. Anxiety takes over and he determines a plan overcome the problem and prevent what he knows would send him into depression unless he acts with finality.'

'Does that excuse him?'

'It is an excuse but not one to overcome his guilt. Look at the planning, the execution of the plan and the resumption of his normal life. Hillary, I think we are dealing with a very disturbed man and like it or not I need to bring him to justice, not only to tie up my Boss's loose ends but to bring closure to everything we have read so far.'

'Changing the subject slightly, Mike, do you think Albert is feeding you the story that he wants. He's certainly drawing you in deeper and deeper. However, any logic that I know follows events chronologically. Simkins would have presented his diaries in that way starting with his birth and so on. What we are getting from Albert is much more random. The last one was an early one. Others we have read are much more recent. Is that significant?

'I assume he has the whole story up to Penfold. That is where I came in. I was fed that because I asked. The Parsons' affair was linked directly to Albert's downfall as a police officer. I understand why both of these were given to me. The other two, Harris and the Headmaster, I think were added to give credence to the fact that Albert believed we were dealing with a dangerous killer and also, he knew that I, sorry, we would uncover more than maybe he could.

'Still think there's more to it, Mike.'

Chapter 20

Robbie – Sadness and Loss

Session 7 Part 1

'I fancy we should spend the night in?'

'Agreed. Take away, bottle of wine and a classic movie?'

'OK, I'll deal with the first two, you surf the TV. Your choice, I won't argue.'

It was just past 10pm, when Mike's laptop sprung into life.

**

'How are you today, Brian?'

'I'm fine. A little less bright, if you want the absolute truth. Anyway, shall we begin?'

'This is a strange title.'

'Yes, but that is how I felt about the whole episode.' I let her read on.

Back then in the late 1960s very few of us had transport of our own, but Robbie did. His father had bought him a yellow sports car, that became the envy of us all and he knew it. His father had been awarded a CBE in the Queen's birthday honours and Robbie was at pains to remind us as often as he could. I felt sorry for him as he was clearly a sensitive child overawed by a dominant father who expected much of him. He wasn't the brightest button on the blouse, but he had immense charm, life and soul of a party of which there were many that first term.

Like me he endured boarding school and survived. This, we had in common, and, in the early days, it bound us together. I did not mind covering lectures for him. In an unwritten rule, early morning lectures were to be covered by me as he had great difficulty in getting out of bed before noon. It didn't matter whether it was his own bed or some lady's.'

Barbara looked up. 'It sounds to me that you had an envy button pressed inside you.'

'Barbara, that's probably true, at least at first. It was his casual approach to every aspect of his life and a magnetism that seemed to attract every woman that came within his sphere of influence.' She looked down at my diary.

In return for my lecture notes, on days at weekends, in his yellow sports car, wind whistling through our hair, he drove to anywhere that took our fancy always returning for some party or other. "Father pays all this," as he waved his hand in the air with another lunch bill, which, of course, I already knew. I'd come to realise that his main problem was that he never seemed to engage with other people. His existence was all so superficial.

Yes, everyone knew about him, but it never occurred to him that other people had stories to tell. Intimacy was something he hid behind his façade of bonhomie.

Barabara looked up again. 'Did it occur to you that maybe you saw something of yourself in him?'

'I did wonder if I were the same.'

I was curious to know what he was afraid of. Whilst he looked, with his blond hair and slate grey eyes, our age, I found out that he was five years older. What had happened in those five years? Was he hanging onto a secret?

"You can smell it." She read the words aloud and looked at me across the coffee table.

'Barbara, those were the words that were to change everything between Robbie and me.'

'I see.'

Crime was one of the four new subjects that second year. In front of us, our lecturer, was an ex-copper, Detective Inspector Simon Jenkins explaining his experiences when investigating the uncomfortable subject of allegations of Incest. Robbie was clearly uncomfortable, shifting in his seat, hand wavering over his notepad, head down. I could see that he'd written nothing on the page, I watched Robbie, at the end of the lecture, as he strode out without a backward glance. I clearly thought I had witnessed something strange. I had to find out more.

'Did you?' she asked. This was turning into a "question and answer" session.

'Please read on. It is all there in the diary. Yes, a great deal more.'

DI Jenkins suggested when I asked him about the psychology of the criminal mind that there was a book written by a colleague of his, Anthony Ruthin, based in the North of England, Yorkshire Constabulary with a chapter on the subject in our library.

In Chapter 5, there was a story about a family whose lives had been turned upside down by an unexpected death. I wondered if I'd be able to justify my feelings of dread should I find Robbie amongst these pages or was I just reading all the wrong signs that I had seen in Robbie's face. I became lost in time, afternoon drifted into early evening. I missed a lecture on Company Law. Lights were switched on as darkness fell outside. I couldn't take my eyes from the pages until one sentence stopped me in my tracks, "teenagers are always the most difficult to read, emotionally they are disturbed by their own feelings, never quite knowing what is right or wrong."

I turned to the beginning of this story; it was headed "Sadness and Loss". The events were set in Sheffield, some years ago. The case involved a wealthy family living in a large mansion outside the city in open countryside. Father had his own steel company, inherited from his own father. He was described as a domineering workaholic. Mother looked after all the domestic arrangements, a good host to all the father's many business connections. Did I begin to associate this with what I knew about Robbie? Maybe, as he did not talk about his life at home, only small snippets emerging now and again particularly when he had

had too much to drink, but I had a picture of his parents in my mind and the description fitted.

There had been a death in the family. Robbie had told me that his elder sister, Rona, had died. She was a couple of years his senior and he worshipped her. In this story I was reading, Samantha had fallen from a sixth-floor balcony of her university flat in London. Initially, the police reported that it had been an accident as her blood alcohol levels were very high and they assumed it had impeded her balance. The shocking discovery was that she was three months pregnant, and nobody had been aware. Now the police were considering that her death was suicide, although there was no evidence that Samantha had known she was carrying a child.

Samantha's father had brought his influence to bear on the tragedy. Calls were made and in deference to the family and his standing as part of the industrial establishment and as there were apparently no other people involved, it was generally accepted that alcohol was the overriding factor in her death. Clearly the story did not stop there as I concentrated on the rest of the chapter. I looked at my watch. Plenty of time to finish.

What was not revealed to the police or the coroner, before the verdict of misadventure, was a letter that had arrived several days after Samantha's death at the family home addressed to her younger brother, Alex. Here, I was certain the Ruthin story was the real-life events of my friend

Robbie. As I read on, I substituted Samantha for Rona and Alex for Robbie in the story and continued to read. Robbie recognised Rona's handwriting and ran to his room to open the envelope. Having read the contents, he remained there for hours fingering the paper with her last words written so matter-of-factly, stating her reasons for taking her own life and saving her father from humiliation. She had talked to no-one about her condition and had internalised the whole situation until depression had taken hold of her and she slipped beyond the point of redemption.

I recognised what must have been a desolate place in which she found for herself. Years earlier a friend of mine with three children asked me to meet him for a drink one evening. He had been helping me with some house renovations and wanted to discuss the work. I did not think anything unusual. He seemed in good spirits. The next day, I received a call from his wife that he had taken an overdose that wasn't fatal as he left that morning in his car, and she'd called the police when he hadn't turned up to his day job and she was very worried. It was then that I realised the significance of parts of our conversation. He had been making sure that I would be there for his family when….

Barbara stopped reading and looked up with concern written over her face.

'Brian, these calls for help are impossible to detect especially when someone has made up their mind such as your friend. You mustn't carry blame.'

'Easier said than done. Anyway, he was found a day later in a remote spot having inhaled carbon monoxide from the car exhaust. His wife couldn't summon the courage to identify him, would I do so at the hospital? On my arrival, I was shown into a small room painted shabbily in light green with a small table, littered with well fingered magazines, mostly advertising funeral directors' services. I had barely sat down when an elderly man in white overalls ushered me into an adjoining room. In the middle, was a trolley with my friend's body covered with a white sheet. He pulled back the sheet from his face, before me was a pale, calm image, his brown hair dishevelled. I nodded recognition, asking myself why they hadn't combed his hair to match his white collar and tie.'

She had listened to me without interrupting seeing that I was still troubled by the situation but went back to my diary.

'So, in this scenario of Ruthin's words, you became obsessed that you were reading about Robbie's family history?'

'Yes, I was certain.'

'Despite his outward show of confidence, I got the distinct feeling that he could not let go of the letter or the feeling of responsibility. I imagined him clinging to the letter, alone in his bedroom, each night, remembering her smell and her touch. It was impossible for him to think rationally. There was no-one in the family that he could talk to. His father was too busy in his business. His mother kept up her pretence that all was well, never considering what affect the loss of Rona would have on Robbie. We have all got to move on, was the only solution. I could imagine his confusion and stress.'

'You could see yourself suffering as he did?'

'Especially with what happened next.' I pointed to the diary.

Robbie's behaviour signalled that something was very wrong. At the time, his parents assumed it was a late reaction to Rona's death, so did the staff at school. According to Ruthin's story Robbie's actions went beyond the norm. His secret developed into its own trauma. He became its prisoner, hidden behind its steel bars. He made himself a victim and as such chose to fight. He had uncontrolled episodes of violence, destroying school property, but not understanding why. His actions were unpredictable and dangerous. His school decided it could cope no longer and he was asked to leave. His parents didn't know what to do. They were now losing their only son.'

I imagined their sense of hopelessness. I assumed a private psychiatric clinic was the only solution. His father signed his son into their care, not wanting to know anything about the treatments his son was about to endure. I'm putting words into his mouth, but I can imagine he told them to just "fix" his son. As he joined me at University, I had to assume the clinic did succeed in rehabilitating him, but they couldn't have overcome the facts merely put them into context so that he could deal with them on a day-to-day basis with gradual acceptance.

According to Ruthin's book, a letter arrived addressed to the investigating officer quoting the case reference for Rona's suicide file. It was marked "private and confidential" and there was no return address but was post-marked "Haversham, Buckinghamshire". For these details to be on the envelope was unusual so DI Ransome took the precaution of donning a pair of gloves and slit open the envelope, inside was a hand-written letter, the ink had faded, and it was obvious it had been handled many times, but it was quite capable of being read. If this story was about Robbie, as I read the heavily redacted one reproduced, I was now certain I was right. His reaction during the lecture and quick departure afterwards confirmed this in my mind.

XXXXXXXXXXXXXXXXXX, when you read this, I'll be gone. Don't blame yourself but I know you probably will. It was my fault. XXXXXXXXXXXX it was just you and me, we had no-one else to love us. XXXXXXXXXXXXXXXXXXXXXXXXXXX together through the holidays, enjoying our freedom. We were both curious

XXXXXXXXXXXXXXX. It didn't feel wrong. XXXXX.

The rest of the letter was left by Ruthin to the reader's imagination, covered in Xs. The police investigation was not re-opened officially. Handwriting experts differed in their opinion, but two out of three confirmed it was that of Rona. The police were aware of the subsequent breakdown of her brother, Robbie, as their colleagues had noted the file following his behaviour both at school and subsequently in Sheffield where he'd been out in the early hours of the morning intoxicated and stumbling around and on the last occasion, he'd become violent and had to be constrained by police officers and taken home. At last, his mother realised that his state of mind was causing the family too much embarrassment and that sooner rather than later, he would be in serious trouble. He needed help that they were not equipped to provide it, so he was taken into the care of a clinic.

DI Ransome decided that, even though Robbie was still a juvenile in the eyes of the law. He would advise Robbie's psychiatrist, as the appropriate adult, of his proposed visit even though technically he need not be present when they met, he would insist. Thereby avoiding any confrontation later on with Robbie's father.

**

'You'll find him quite well now, Inspector. He has made remarkable progress since he was admitted. Remarkable. He still refuses to see his parents, but I am sure that will change. Come, I will introduce you. He told me that you would be coming. He's expecting you, although I have no idea how he knew?'

'I think I do, Doctor.'

'Here we are,' said Doctor Greenfield.'

'I've been expecting you. Had a few hurdles to jump through first, I expect?'

'The usual protocols. I've asked Doctor Greenfield to stay if you have no objection?'

'No, we get on well, don't we, Doctor?'

Greenfield nodded.

'Please sit.'

'Can I assume that you sent this anonymous envelope?'

'Yes, with the letter inside.'

'When did you actually receive it?'

'A few days after my sister fell from the balcony of her flat in London. I assume she sent it beforehand knowing what she intended to do.'

'It would have been a vital piece of evidence to establish, suicide, don't you agree?'

'Yes, I understand that but…..'

'But what?' Ransome hesitated. Doctor Greenfield was not privy to the contents. and he hoped that the accusation he was about to make would not send his patient spiralling out of control again but if that was the case, he'd concluded, why send the letter in the first place.

'Nothing.'

'Do you realise that this,' he held the letter out, 'seems to confirm that you and your sister had sexual relations. That is a serious offence. Have you got anything to say about that?'

Doctor Greenfield leaned forward and placed his hand on Robbie's arm uncertain whether to allow this interview to continue, but Robbie shrugged him off violently.

His voice was raised a few notches as he said, 'Is that what you think those words mean, Inspector?'

'I have no doubt.'

'The case is closed. Misadventure. That letter confirms her intention to end her own life. You said so yourself.'

'The case can be re-opened with this letter and more importantly we must remember that she wasn't the only one to die. She was carrying a child. Can I assume it was your child?'

Robbie opened his arms in supplication. He had reached the end of a long road of guilt. Now finally, was his chance to rid himself of those demons inside and by sending the letter, he had chosen to do so. It must have been a difficult decision but how else was he going to be able to move forward. What came next surprised me.'

'Rona was being kind to me in that letter. She knew I had made her suffer and she didn't want me to be in pain for the rest of my life, so she took some blame for what happened between us. It was not consensual. I was a brute that day. I was much stronger than her. I did not stop myself. Our relationship changed. Looking back since I've been here, I think she wrote that letter so that I would never forget what I'd done and knowing the hurt it would cause.'

**

Ransome watched Robbie's face in the silence that followed as tears fell down Robbie's cheeks.

'For Rona, I doubted it. For himself, I was sure. He had got away with it. In my eyes, he might as well have pushed her and her unborn child off the balcony that day. He was relying on being forgiven. DI Ransome never filed a further report. The letter was placed in the closed file, "no further action."'

'Brian what was your reaction?'

'I was livid. It seemed so unjust that he was just able to feel contrite and walk away, I was drained. I wondered how many other girls had been subjected to his mastery of charm and found themselves with a tender hand clamped over their mouths. As I lay awake that night, I wrestled with the question of how I was to confront him and find out whether Ruthin's story was really about him. The next day gave me my opportunity as he handed me a copy of the notes, he had taken in my absence from the Company Law lecture. I told him I was waylaid in the library and now an expert on Incest cases and related the Ruthin case story. I watched his reaction, his facial expression, as I tapped my briefcase indicating the notes I had supposedly taken. His face darkened and he turned away momentarily.'

Chapter 21

London and Cardiff South Wales Next Day

'Well, so much for a good film.'

'Would have been if you'd turned off that damned machine!'

'Thought I had, but nevertheless I didn't, so where are we now.'

'Tell ex-DI Thornton not to post things on Sunday nights.' Mike laughed at the thought.

'Looks like another situation that Simkins is about to take into his own hands.'

'Feels like that. I agree.'

'Do you get the impression that Albert's report is only part of a session? asked Hillary.'

'Maybe. It certainly only half a story.'

'Maybe they ran out of the allotted session time.'

'Or, perhaps, Albert is dragging you in a little more.'

'Indeed, my dear lady,' said Mike with a conciliatory smile, 'and needs me to find out if there's any truth in the matter. Looks like a trip to Cardiff tomorrow, but first I need to report to Roger Simmons. Hillary, can you do some digging whilst I'm at the office? We'll go down on the late morning train. Roger likes his meeting early or late, so I'll surprise him tomorrow, never thinks I get up before mid-morning.'

'You want me to find out about Rona?'

'Yes, please. Night cap?

Mike poured two brandies and sat back savouring the ethereal, pungent and earthy aroma with his arm around Hillary's shoulder, trying desperately to keep his eyes from closing and stifling a yawn.

'Bored are we, Mike?'

'No, just exhausted. Remember you kept me up late for the last two nights!'

'I thought it was a mutual decision.'

'It was a delightful mutual decision. Come on let's try to sleep tonight, young lady.'

**

'Sir, there's not too much to report just yet. I have some interesting leads, but I am dealing with an unusual suspect and a contact that I am weary of, to say the least. One lead, in particular, that is taking me to Cardiff later this morning,' said Mike to an attentive Roger Simmons.

'You want to elaborate on your contact?'

'Not at this stage, save to say that all of the evidence he is providing is unusable in a court of law because of the way it has been obtained.'

'Illegal surveillance?'

'Yes. I know I should be used to it, but this is giving me ethical anguish.'

'Make sure you have the edge, just in case.'

'I have enough to stay clean.'

'Good, just keep me posted on your progress. By the way, I hear you are spending time with Ms Barnes again. How was Paris?'

'Yes, and how did you know about Paris?'

'Our man at the Embassy flagged your arrival and wanted to know if you were on official business. I told him you were taking time off. I assume that was correct?'

'Absolutely, Hillary is now unemployed and back in London. For your information, she's staying in my apartment, looking in due course for another job. Any vacancies here at the Circus?' said Mike laughing.'

Roger Simmons ignored the question. An interesting thought, he tucked away for later, maybe.

'Glad to hear, Michael. You need a good woman by your side. So, Cairo's under the bridge?'

'Well and truly.'

'Good. Haven't mentioned it before but Colonel Nassar has recommended Hillary for some sort of Gallantry medal for her involvement in bringing the Denshawai case to a close.'

'Not sure she'd appreciate the reminder of her own mortality.'

'She can pin it on the wall for her children.'

Mike stood, smiling at the thought and bade Roger goodbye. He met Hillary at Paddington station and they boarded the 10.50 to Cardiff. As they settled into their first-class seats, Hillary took out a bundle of papers from her briefcase and handed them to Mike.

'Can you preçis them for me?' asked Mike

'I started with an application to the Statutory Register in Edinburgh. Births, deaths and marriages had been centralised there since 1855

'Enlightened lot these Scots,' said Mike.

'We had part of her full name, so I eventually found a Rona McFee Alexandria Grant, approximate year of birth and death. I was surprised by the speed that the certified copy arrived by email. Used your account. The first fact that surprised was the cause of death.

'It was stated that a Fatal Accident enquiry had been launched by the Scottish Procurator Fiscal under the 1895 Act. The cause of death was, "Trauma Brain Injury. Consistent with falling from a great height. Took her own life."

'This was consistent with the Ruthin's story, although her death was in Scotland, not London. There was no mention of alcohol and no possibility that it was an accident? asked Mike.'

'No. Where does this get us?'

'It tells us that what Simkins was telling Dr Carling was true to the extent that he was there at the same time as Robbie Grant and had cause to suspect Robbie was the reason for his sister's suicide.'

'There is little chance of being able to confirm that he had been committed into psychiatric care unless I get MI6 to force the release of their patient's confidential papers. Probably not a road to go down at this stage and I don't think Roger would sanction the request. Too much paper. That's all?'

Maybe we wait and see if there is a follow up from Albert. That may save you using vital resources in your office. For the moment, let's see what Cardiff unearths for us. By the way, Mike, you're seeing a Dr Reece Williams at the University when we arrive.'

'That's very efficient of you.'

'Actually, I introduced myself to Professor Paul Mitchell. Seems a lovely guy. Said a lot of good things about you. He made the introduction for you.'

'I pay him well!'

After a light train lunch, they decided to walk from the station along St Mary's Street where Mike left Hillary to window gaze as he continued into Cathays Park and the Registrar's office.

'Thank you for seeing me at such short notice, Dr Williams.'

'Reece, please, Michael. No problem.' I have read the email. Interesting line of work,'

'Can be if you don't mind the hours.'

'Well, I have the records here for those years. The 1960s is a long time ago to be still searching for something or someone, if I may say so.'

'Reece, we lost a man some time ago in what may or may not be suspicious circumstances. I'm just preparing a report on background and contacts to see where it leads.' Mike was scanning the records as coffee arrived.

'Thanks. Reece, hope I'm not stopping you from other important matters.'

'Not at all.' He picked up a letter from the in-tray and started to read.

Mike suddenly, put the cup down and started scribbling notes furiously. Reece watched intently.

'Found something of interest?'

'Maybe. Is Detective Inspector Simon Jenkins still around? One of the law lecturers in the late 1960s.'

'No. He'd be long gone by now. Retired the year after I came, 1980, I think.'

'Shame, I'd liked to have met him.' Mike continued making further notes then thanked Reece for his time. He met Hillary who by now was carrying several bags. He took them from her, and she linked arms as they strolled back to the station.

In the carriage speeding back to London, Mike handed his notes to Hillary then opened the laptop. He requested a copy of Robbie Grant's death certificate, a copy of the Coroner's report and the archived file containing the Police investigation.

'Your writing is terrible, but I think I have got the gist. I am assuming you beginning to feel that this is another Simkins murder.'

'Afraid so, but until we get the other papers I've just requested, you are right, it's just a feeling.'

Chapter 22

Dr Carling's Consulting Rooms

Session 7 Part II

Not long after Mike and Hillary had settled down after their trip to South Wales and were sitting relaxing with a half full bottle of French white Bordeaux sitting in front of them on the table, Mike's laptop pinged. Albert's next follow up, preceded by the words, "Any joy in Cardiff?"

'Bloody hell, Mike. He's watching us as well!'

Mike did not answer. He was reading the next diary intently.

**

'Brian, why did you feel that it was your duty to carry on this exploration into Robbie's past?

'That's just the way I am wired. Once I am irritated by a lack of justice, I cannot let go. I needed him to admit that was partly where five years of his late teenage life were spent?'

'Did you succeed?'

'Yes, it occurred soon after the beginning of the next term. As always, the first few days were ones of re-adjustment usually accompanied by sessions of alcohol abuse. It was sometime after midnight, and we were both a little worse for wear when I took him to one side from the others who littered themselves around the flat.

'Robbie, something has been bothering me,' I said deliberately slurring my words.

'Umm, and what can that be?'

'Well, you're older than most of us and I'm wondering why you left it so late to study law. Did you go travelling or did you work?'

'He looked at me through bleary eyes "Promise not to tell?" he said, quietly.

'Why should I if it's a secret? Promise.'

'After Rona died, I had a bad time, really bad.' He was slurring his words and looking at my face trying to focus. I had to lean into him to catch the words. 'My parents couldn't control the person I was becoming so they had me locked away until I was better.'

'I'm sorry but you're OK now,' I managed as he slumped back and began to snore.

Next day, I wondered if Robbie would remember our conversation and I really had no idea what, if anything, I should do. I began to wonder, as DI Ransome and the Psychiatrist, had concluded, that Robbie had completely recovered from his ordeal. He was charming and charismatic, but I was fearful that he had crafted this front and that underneath, he had learned nothing from his experience and that he was the same person who had raped his sister and got away with it.

'During that term, I met Annie, the person I was to spend the rest of my life with. Robbie was disenchanted that I was spending more time with her than him. He seemed unhappy and a little lost. I had not abandoned him, but he may have felt that I had.

'You're too young to be settling down. Come on, there's still time for that, we're here to have fun.'

'We do,' I replied, trying to lighten his mood. 'But it's OK to have a steady girlfriend?'

'Sure. Just don't get too close, too soon, you'll miss all the fun.'

'In my absence at half term, Robbie had tried on several occasions to use his charm to encourage Annie to go out with him. She had rebuffed him on each occasion but on his last try, he had become more assertive, holding her tightly and trying to kiss her but she'd managed to fight him off. She became afraid of him and told me that she did not feel comfortable in his presence.

'After his latest attempt, she'd talked to a few of her friends who'd fallen for Robbie's charms, and whilst there were no allegations of rape, a few girls had failed to stop him and had eventually given in under duress, according to the hushed talk amongst her house mates.

'I told her not to worry, now that I was back. I would solve the issue. I tried to avoid him as much as possible. My relationship with Robbie became more distant and strained. I knew he was potentially a sick bastard."

**

‘I asked you last time we met, “do you feel intense distress when something reminds you of your traumatic past, whether you think about it or something in you sees it.”

‘I remember saying, “Wow, that’s a difficult one”.’

‘I also recall that was your response. Well, after a week’s thought, what do you think?’

‘Whatever is hidden deep inside, I can only say it is an intense distress signal that is mirrored by my actions. Sometimes, I see it or imagine it, other times I think about it.’

‘So, in what I have just heard about Robbie, I can see that you were beginning to feel stress from observing his reaction during that first lecture. Did that relate back in any way?’

‘Not immediately, at that point I had an uncomfortable feeling, not distressed. Only later, as I dug into his past, did “uncomfortable” turn to distress. I imagined the physical sensation of the touch of his strong arms on an unwilling recipient. It stimulated my own uncomfortable experience and my subjective familiarity with that emotion at the time. Does that make sense?’

‘Yes, so it was a feeling of intense distress that built up inside your head?’

‘I could acutely imagine seeing Rona fighting off her brother, the physical struggle to survive intact.’

‘Despite what had happened, I did thank Robbie for Annie’s birthday present and laughed off his primitive joke of the sending her frilly underwear. It was now all part of my strategy to ensure trust was re-established.

'You know I was only kidding. My sad sense of humour. She was never interested in me.'

'It's OK. Perhaps I should have come around to your place and given you a good hiding!'

'Not in you, I know that but let us pretend you did, and I've now recovered. Fancy a day out, just had the car serviced so should be good to go.'

'I imagined this day would arrive. So many events led to it. Rona's death, Robbie's continued inability to recognize that he was a danger to others and finally his complete disregard of my relationship with Annie.

'On this drive out of town north into the wilds of the Wye valley, after lunch, I insisted on driving back. It was a bright day although cold. The previous night it had snowed, and it still remained on the ground in shaded areas. There was a threat of more to come.

'I was reminded sitting in the dining room years ago in 1958 when news came in of the plane crash that decimated the Manchester United football team at Munich airport when snow and ice gathered on the wings and inhibited take-off lift. It crashed into the snow-covered field beyond the runway. I needed to know exactly what happened and who was responsible. Was it a catalogue of small errors leading to the catastrophe? The course of events that it conjured in my mind were helped by Robbie being inebriated and asleep beside me. Whilst there were no regulations in force against drink driving, it was clear to me that day, he was incapable of avoiding trouble if he took the wheel. As darkness fell, I drove into his same parking space as always and pushed the little car further forward than usual and onto the downward slope of the snow-covered grass under the trees that had not seen the sunlight that day. Whatever happened next, I would never feel the sorrow for what I did that night.'

Dr Carling continued to look down at the diary, fingering the pages, not daring to catch Brian Simkins' eyes. She felt a distinct unease about this old man in front of her, but she was a professional and had a job to do.

Tony's last page before he went to hospital. 02.22.

Chapter 23

Present Day - Mike's Apartment

Robbie Grant's Death Certificate confirmed the cause of death as drowning. The Coroner's Report concluded that he had consumed a great deal of alcohol that according to the pathologist's evidence would have severely inhibited his ability to stand let alone drive a vehicle. Several publicans gave evidence of Robbie and Simkins being in their pubs. Simkins admitted he had had to drive back to Cardiff as Robbie was too drunk to drive safely. After reading that Mike turned to Hillary.

'That begs the question how did Robbie manage to get into the driver's seat, turn on the ignition and misjudge reverse for first gear in his own car like that? The tyre marks wouldn't have registered in any other gear than first, save maybe second.'

'Simkins said he'd left Robbie getting something he thought maybe be an umbrella from the boot, but he couldn't be sure as he had already walked out of the carpark on his way home and the street lighting was feeble.'

'Another bizarre method of operation?'

'True, but these MOs are his signature. They are unlike anything else we've been taught. Convicted serial killers work the same method every time. Jack the Ripper, offering to pay for sex, would lure his victims into a secluded street or square and then slice their throats. As the women rapidly bled to death, he would then brutally disembowel them with the same six-inch knife. Look at Ted Bundy for example, he typically strangled or bludgeoned his victims as well as mutilating them after death.'

'Okay, Mike, I get what you are saying.'

'Linked with Simkins' bizarre MOs, there is his unusual selection process. Whilst I am not condoning what he has allegedly done, the victims are all personal to him, but he also believes that he is saving others from some future fate he would rather not contemplate for them.'

'What did Albert say to you?'

Mike thought back to his second meeting at The Royal Oak with Albert. 'I think his words were "Kept banging on about needing police type vigilantes", or something like that.'

'Some vigilante, hey?'

The intercom buzzed. Mike and Hillary set aside Albert's latest report from Dr Carling's office containing the conclusion of Simkins's continued conversational session with her about his relationship with Robbie Grant and the diary.

'I'll be down immediately,' answered Mike. He returned with a special delivery parcel, he ripped it open and spread the file on the table. Hillary sat next to him as they read the contents.

The Police had traced the cars last known position on the snow-packed ice on the carpark verge adjacent to the banks of the river. Black and white photographs showed tyre marks on the tarmac where they had gripped the surface. The freezing weather had preserved the car's path through the snow before it plunged over the bank into the river. The only witness to those last minutes was Brian Simkins. He told them that Robbie was still drowsy despite sleeping all the way back from the last pub. He had left the car with the hand brake on but couldn't remember what gear if any he'd left the car in. When it was suggested that he may have driven into the parking space in first gear, he could not recall.

When asked why he left the scene before Robbie, he had told them that he had much further to walk home, and he was cold and wet. Did he recall hearing the car revving loudly? No. Did he see anything unusual? No. The streetlights across the road hardly made any impression on the shadows engulfing the little car. There was nobody around. He had pulled his scarf and collar higher against the strengthening flurries of snow and the biting cold wind that gusted across the carpark.

'Nothing much else. Without a face-to-face confession, we only have our suspicions again, but we need to finish Albert's latest. Maybe, just maybe, there's something we can hang our hat on'

**

Barbara Carling eventually looked up and across at Simkins.

'I'm beginning to feel a little awkward here, Brian. 'Your behaviour is producing a clear pattern. I am certain that it could have been broken years ago if maybe you had received proper help, then. Do you see that?'

'Yes, I am beginning see that, but nobody was aware of my behaviour, save me. Are you suggesting that with a burgeoning career in law ahead that I'd walk into a lunatic asylum?'

'No. That would have been inappropriate and unhelpful.

'You can see that Robbie was the same person before help was sought for him as he was afterwards. It did not work for him. No treatment worked in those days. Understanding on the human mind was in its infancy compared to today. Look at your retrospective thoughts on PTSD that we are going through now.'

Barbara Carling was determined to seize the opportunity to put Simkins on the spot. Not let him hide amongst the rest of the population.

'Did you recognize that you were doing something that was wrong at a very basic level?'

'Wrong?

'Legally or morally? I agree that some well-meaning people say, "it's never right to kill." I have always been a pacifist but accept that my stance may be because I have never had to go to war. Therefore, I have never had to question my viewpoint. I am saddened by the fact that killing each other, as history shows us, is part of the human experience and mankind has always had a fascination with it.'

'Brian, you are missing my point here. I'm talking about you, not those nations or peoples.'

'I am sorry, Barbara but, I do not see the difference? That is the pivotal question. Look at the Haitian sugar cane slave rebellion of 1781, for example. Their success by peaceful means, by withdrawing the labour or forming a union to fight their demands, would have resulted in a massacre by the French. Far fewer were killed in their physical fight for justice. Appeasement against Hitler and fascism only emboldened his belief that Europe was his for the taking. Putin in Russia is doing exactly the same thing as we sit and watch. Justice requires force to support it and where that fails, violence is required. My actions were my distress avoidance system coming into play, it satisfied and overcame the feelings within me triggered by my past.'

She ticked another box in the PTSD questionnaire.

'How do you feel now looking back at your time with Robbie?'

'Relieved, both then and now. The law was ineffectual. He should have been held to account. On reliving his death when I gave evidence to the Police and in the Coroner's Court, my distress avoidance system came into play. It satisfied and overcame the reminders of the past. Justice had been achieved when he drowned.'

'It wasn't a personal vendetta?'

'It was an act of retribution for Rona and more importantly, protection for those that would inevitably become his future victims. I have read a lot about the subject of rape since and I believe, as I did then, that it was only a matter of time before he drove down the road of committing more serious and devious offences. As you would say yourself, I perceived a pattern of behaviour that would get worse and more violent, that others had sought to cure and believed they had done so.'

**

'Well, that's something new, an act of retribution. Another admission of guilt.'

'I love to get my hands on the actual written diaries, not just Albert's photocopies, that he presents to her each session.'

'Likewise, but so far we have nothing to present to a court. His lawyers would walk all over us. None of Albert's ill-gotten conversations would be allowed. These sessions are privileged and private. What's left, just our confirmation that events took place, and all the Coroner's and Police files have satisfactory verdicts that absolve Simkins of any wrongdoing,' Mike said sadly. 'He is never going to be caught unless he is driven into a corner.'

‘Do you think we need to meet Albert again? You did promise to tell him what you have found out about Simkins, after all.’

‘True, but I should do this alone. I don’t want you involved with him. In any case we need to formulate a plan of action.’

‘That’s fine if you can but I wasn’t suggesting we both go to see Albert. He’s your contact but remember you don’t trust him always to do the right thing.’

‘Point taken.’

Two hours later, Mike sat down next to Albert and savoured the first few mouthfuls of a pint of London Pride ale.

‘Thanks, mate,’ said Mike observing Albert’s new Cartier watch and gold cuffs but saying nothing. Gone was the slightly scruffy attire. This was a new ex-DI Thornton, he had not seen before. It just registered Hillary’s warning.

‘Interesting few days?’

‘Very much so. Opened a few doors.’

‘Come on, tell me more.’

‘This is part payback, Albert. I owed you one and now part is being repaid. Agreed?’ Mike didn’t wait for a response. ‘Our friend Simkins seems to have a very colourful past, just as you suggested. I think that if you’d been backed by your superiors, you’d be a hero now.’

‘You mean my nose smelt a bad smell correctly?’

‘Yes, I do.’

Mike explained what he'd uncovered about the Law student, the Headmaster and the Bully.'

'You mean he is the serial killer I thought he was.'

'Probably.'

'What do you mean, "probably"?'

'Just a thought that a disturbed man with a strange early past, may just be fantasizing about what could have been.'

'Rubbish, Mike. I unearthed credible evidence against him in the deaths of both Parsons and Penfold. You know most of that would stand up the scrutiny.' Mike nodded, just wondering exactly what Albert's ulterior motive was. 'But what do you want to do? After all, you wanted my help with your man, Penfold, didn't you?"

'Albert, we need to bring him out into the open somehow. Your obsession had its merits, but these old cases show a pattern and without a confession, they are both irrelevant and too remote to form part of my Penfold case, so I need to ask you how you survive these days? I assume that your police pension does stretch too far, or maybe you had to forfeit it.'

'Why should my financial position have any relevance?'

'I'm thinking that we need to somehow get him out of his comfort zone, maybe somewhere abroad, maybe. I haven't thought it through yet.'

'You want to know whether I can afford foreign travel on what I get paid for private investigative work, like tracing people and the photography involved. Well, it keeps me away from the Official Receiver in Bankruptcy.'

Mike did not believe that was Albert's only source of income, but he didn't press the matter. Albert, in his turn, did not elaborate on the shadier side that provided him with a tidy sum each month.

'Well, I may be able to shift some expenses your way, unofficially. I cannot be seen, in any way, to be involved in your surveillance techniques if we're going to work together to nail Mr Simkins.'

'My, my, Michael, you are being ethical and downright unethical at the same time.'

Mike shifted uneasily in his chair on hearing those words, but nevertheless took Albert's outstretched hand.

'Albert, you know perfectly well keeping an eye on a suspected murderer based on illegal surveillance, would be impossible to authorize.'

'Michael, I have the necessary human resources to cover a loner 24/7 if you can assist with a little cash.'

'I think we can assume he works alone. The diary evidence so far confirms this.'

'Right then, I want chapter and verse about what he does each day and where he goes.'

'And what will you be doing in the meantime?'

'MI6 planning and operational skills.'

'Sounds grandiose and bullshit at the same time.'

'No seriously, Albert, to trap someone with his undoubted skills in covering his tracks and avoiding you, will take some unusual planning. I already have some ideas in mind but wanted you on board first. Remember surveillance only. We'll meet here again in two weeks.'

**

Mike left Albert nursing his third Guinness and reported to Roger Simmons at MI6 Headquarters.

'I've read your latest report on Penfold and agree that we don't have enough evidence for the Met to bring the case to court.'

'Apart from you and I, does anyone else know we're searching for Penfold's investigation notes?'

'No, Sir. Anything further from the tech boys that you asked to revisit the case?'

Roger Simmons had withheld information from Mike last time they discussed the computer but now decided to reveal more details.

'We know his own stand-alone computer at Garth Richards, not part of main server, may have hacked. A sophisticated job, so I am advised. Mike, we use hackers who are off-limits. They are considered some of the best in the business in the grey underworld of digital infiltration. Normally they sell to the highest bidder, but our man doesn't need to do that as he's already pretty well off.'

Roger Simmons hesitated. Could his man, whoever he was, have gone rogue? He pushed the thought aside.

'What his name, maybe I can talk to him?'

'I have no idea. All I know is that in some instances he a vital cog in our wheel and if anyone is able to retrieve Penfold's research, it will be him. All I know is that he lives in Spain.'

Momentarily, Mike recalled the Simkins diary: "*Penfold had left his office in a hurry as if he was late for a meeting.*" Had he used this mysterious hacker that Roger Simmons had just mentioned to gain further vital information for MI6's case against Garth Richards. It was possible, after all, Penfold was a forensic accountant not a cyber expert.

Finally. Mike said, 'We need to find him, Sir. Is it possible he's gone rogue with what he's found?'

'No, Michael, he's not that stupid,' said Roger Simmons, but had Mike hit a nerve or suggested something Roger was not comfortable with. Penfold's information was a very valuable asset that others, to protect their anonymity, may be prepared to pay a great deal more than MI6 could afford.

Chapter 24

The Brain Injury

'While you were at Headquarters, a new transcript came in from Albert. Simkins must have arranged a midweek appointment with Dr Carling, unless Albert held this back for some reason. It is very interesting from a psychological point of view. Here read it, whilst I cook us something Russian. They do have some really good food, surprisingly.'

Mike sat down and picked up the script, having poured himself a glass of wine.

**

'Anyway, I have something very interesting to show you.' Simkins delved into his briefcase and pulled out several glossy photographs and turned them towards her. 'What do you see?'

'Brain scan pictures.'

'From a CAT scan. They are showing parts of my brain. Picked them up from the hospital two days ago.'

'Why?'

'You set me thinking about Harris and what your colleagues, Dr Pike, had told you, so I did my own research and spoke to my Oncologist, Raymond Childs, who gave me these. Nothing to do with my cancer, but they looked all over me, just to be certain.'

'So, what does they tell me?

'Raymond told me there was an irregularity in, what he called,' Sinkins looked at his notes, 'the amygdala. It was sunken, and the striatum enlarged.'

'Did he say anything else?'

'Just asked if I had ever had a head injury. Told me, not to worry. It didn't have anything to do with my diagnosis.'

'What did you tell him?'

'Said I had been knocked out twice playing rugby at school.'

'You've only mentioned the Harris kick before. There was another time?'

'Yes. I had not taken too much notice as it was a pure accident, but it did happen. I was not allowed to play for a while. Second year in senior school, I think.'

'Brian, I am very interested in what you just told me. May I have these? I'm due in hospital for some sessions tomorrow. I'll come back to you on these.'

'Sure, you keep them.'

Two days later Dr Carling spoke to Brian by telephone.

'The scan, Brian. I spoke to Raymond and mentioned our discussion. He put me through to Professor Ingram who explained that your sunken amygdala is a brain region responsible for regulating our perceptions of, and reactions to aggression and fear. He postulated that these reactions may have become impaired. He also talked about the enlarged Striatum. Your numerous cognitive, emotional, and motor functions rely on the integrity of the striatum and again he said…..'.'

'Okay, okay,' interrupted Brian. 'If they are respectively sunken and enlarged, what does that actually mean, Barbara?'

'These two concussion incidents are likely to have caused impairment to your emotions and thus your judgements in given circumstances. They both occurred after your birth trauma, so they do not affect our PTSD "experiment", as you like to call it. However, we will need to take them into account when analysing your subsequent behaviour.

**

'Well, what do you think?' said Hillary from the kitchen.

'Not really much the wiser. However, coupled with the possibility of a complete denial, the possible PTSD suffered and this, I think it would be impossible to get a jury to convict him. More likely that he'd be classified as unfit to plead.'

'What does that mean exactly, Mike?'

'If the issue of fitness to plead is raised, a judge may be able to find a person unfit to plead. This is usually done based on information following a psychiatric evaluation. In England and

Wales, the legal test of "fitness to plead" is based their ability to comprehend the course of proceedings in the trial, so as to make a proper defence; or to know that they might challenge any jurors to whom they may object; or to comprehend the evidence; or to give proper instructions to their lawyers.'

'That's very precise!'

'That's because I'm reading it from here.' Hillary joined Mike as he pointed to the computer screen. Further, Hillary, if the issue is raised by the defence, it need only be proved on the balance of probabilities that Simkins is unfit to plead.'

'From his Defence team it would be a very strong argument and that would probably succeed.'

'Indeed, but we know that would be a failure of justice remembering none of our evidence is as yet presentable,' replied Mike letting out a tired sigh of resignation.

'Nothing is proved yet, Mike, we still need to keep him under surveillance and pounce when we can.'

'I will have to ask Roger, now we have this new evidence. He may think otherwise, although I will try to persuade him not to. I am too involved now to let this whole matter go.'

'Well, you can leave that until tomorrow. Sit down and we'll savour some flavours from your Russian kitchen,' said Hillary placing the tureen between them and stirring the contents.

'Remember the note I sent you from Kiev, Mike?'

'Yes. I recognise the colour you described.'

'Borscht. I've dulled it somewhat as I remember you weren't too enamoured with beetroot. Here sprinkle this dill and a spoonful of sour cream, you'll love it.'

Mike did as he was told and tentatively put a spoon full to his mouth. 'What else have you laced this with?'

'Beef, potatoes, carrots and tomatoes.'

'Umm, I approve.' What do you call this?' said Mike pointing to the side salad.

'"Olivier" after the Belgium chef Lucien who worked at the Hermitage. Sorry, I could not find any caviar, grouse, smoked duck or veal tongue in your fridge so I used what I could find. At least you had mayo and a few herbs, beef, eggs, actually one egg, carrots peas and potatoes.'

'If I'd known I would have stopped off at Fortum and Masons on my way back.' Mike uncorked the bottle he'd selected, not knowing it would be a very good complement for the main course, a Northern Spanish country wine made from Grenache grapes and poured Hillary a glass. He held his glass high. 'Nostrovia '

Hillary laughed. 'Not quite right. That means "let's get drunk", Mike!'

'Well, not a bad idea, anyway.' He took a large mouthful and refilled his glass.

So far there had been no mention again of a Simkins, but as Hillary disappeared into the kitchen again with the used plates, Mike ventured a thought.

'If Roger agrees tomorrow, you and I need to put a plan together. Albert's keeping up his vigil and will help.'

'I hope you didn't commit too much. That man worries me.'

Hillary returned to the table and picked up her glass. Next time, the famous Count Alexander Grigorievich Stroganoff dish. Find one of the many global variations that you like best.'

'No need. The strips of fillet beef. My favourite. You cook it the way you want.'

Then the computer whirred into action.

Chapter 25

Some years ago - The Fraudster

Session 8

Annie and I were helping my daughter to buy her own house using some equity in our house to fund the deposit. I advised her to try to undertake the legal process by herself and that I would explain things as she went along. I was unable to undertake the legal work as I was enjoying my comfortable retirement.

She was expecting to exchange contracts and at the sellers' request, complete the transaction, very soon thereafter and had received an email request for funds from her lawyer which both she and I were expecting. She had already sent direct to her lawyers as requested by email, the money for searches. Everyone had been informed that Annie and I were assisting financially. I duly transferred the funds to her Bank as before and she forwarded them on to the Bank detailed on her lawyer's letterheaded email to a solicitors account in their name.

When I asked her days later if there was any news, she rang her solicitor.

'Dad, I'm confused,' she said in a panicked voice later that day.

'What about, darling?'

'They aren't ready and have not asked for any money.'

'But what about their letter.'

'They're saying it wasn't from them and in any case, they are saying they'd never request money by email.'

'Well, that's not true. They asked for the search money by email,' I reminded her.

'Send me all those emails and the Bank details, don't worry I'll sort it.'

Later that night, I sat down trying to get my head around the situation. I was reading through all the correspondence that I had printed out.

'There's a nasty smell here,' I shouted as Annie appeared from the kitchen.

'What?'

'Fraud!' I explained the circumstances in detail as Annie listened.

'What can we do?'

'I don't know yet. I will sleep on it. Too tired tonight.'

'Have we lost all that money?'

'Probably, but I'll find a way out.'

'That's awful.'

All night, until my eyes wouldn't stay open any longer, I tried to figure out who I could hold to account, her email company for lack of protection of their users, the solicitors for failing to have sufficient technology in place to prevent their identity being stolen, my daughter's bank for failing to spot a fraudulent receiver's account or the Bank who took the money on behalf of the fraudster. I was up next morning early, to catch my daughter before she left for work. I had urgent instructions for her.

'Right, darling, don't worry, we'll sort it. Get a pen and paper.' Moments later she was ready.

'First, immediately change your email address and when you've time, tell everyone although that part can wait. Second, phone the Cyber Fraud Squad and tell them what has happened and get a case number. I will send a letter through that you can sign and send on. Thirdly, I have drafted letters to your email service provider, both banks and your lawyers. Print them off, add the Police number, sign them and send special delivery. Then we'll sit back and see what happens.'

'You're a star, Dad. I was so worried.'

'The money's been stolen. Of that I have no doubt, but we'll find some replacement.'

**

Dr Carling broke off her reading and looked across at me

'This is dreadful.'

'And disgusting,' I added, still very angry at what had occurred and the complacency and camouflage that followed from all those so-called honest brokers involved.

'Did you ever recover anything?'

'Nothing.'

'Who do you blame?'

'Initially, the E-Bank in London who received the money, a subsidiary owned by some American giant who denied that their scrutiny systems for new customers setting up accounts was in any way flawed. It was absolute rubbish as they had allowed a bogus solicitors account to be opened in almost the same name as my daughter's solicitors minus the LLP using what must have been some sort of stolen ID and then to operate unchecked and in the blink of an eye it was closed taking our money with it. I still blame them, but to chase our money would have cost five times as much through the courts. Just wasn't worth it in the end and that's what they rely on.'

'I'm sorry,'

'Oh, don't be.' I pointed at the papers she held in her hand. 'I just wish Banks would live up to their old reputation of being honest brokers instead of admitting that they are dishonestly broken.'

**

Through a friend of mine to whom I explained the details, I managed to find the now defunct e-mail and then the domain site of the fraudster. My daughter passed this on to the police and asked if there was any news. I told her not to get excited as they had hundreds of similar cases, most with much higher value than ours. The smaller the amount, usually the lesser attention it receives, unless they can find a linking pattern.

Finally, one and a half years after the event, my daughter received a letter from the police. She rang their office and gave them authority to speak to me. I picked up the phone and rang their number.

'We've been pursuing your daughter's case, but you'll appreciate we have hundreds of complaints to deal with at any one time. We have linked her matter with several others. All I can tell you is that they led to an address in London, Newgate Court. Sorry, but that is still to be followed up after a phone call confirming there was no-one currently registered there with the name we had. All the investigations are still ongoing. Just thought I'd bring you up-to-date.'

'May I ask who you were looking for?'

'You may, but we think it's likely to be an alias, perhaps one of many, hang on a second, Gerard Reynolds.'

The next morning, armed with my file I set out to Newgate Court. It was a far cry from the Victorian debtors' prison, the notorious Newgate goal, built on the old Roman wall in 1188. It was a bleak place for murderers, rapists, debtors and, appropriately fraudsters. Although it was demolished in 1902, even today Newgate Court is cheerless place, exacerbated by the grey skies and misting rain, now surrounded by modern blocks of concrete and glass. I pressed the bell of the serviced office block offering small suites for short-term rent, I shook my umbrella and walked into the reception area. I was not sure whether this was the right place, but my gut instinct told me that the address had the right kind of prestige and the set-up allowed anonymous transient occupation. Great for our fraudster.

'I'm looking to speak to one of your tenants,' I said opening my briefcase.

'Name, please.'

'Mr Gerard Reynolds.'

She looked at her screen,

'Sorry, no-one currently occupying an office here under that name.'

Just as I suspected.

'Look, it is vitally important that I find him. What about previous tenants?'

She got out of her chair beckoning me to sit down. Moments later, she returned with a smartly suited man with smiling face. I stood.

'Morning, my name's Rodney Evans, if you'd like to follow me, Mr Simkins?'

I followed him down a short corridor to a brightly lit office, elegantly furnished with modern light ash veneered desk and matching cabinets. I took my file from my case and opened it on his desk, pulling the chair forward. I explained to him what had happened and how I had been led to his offices. Rodney Evans listened intently, a worried look started to appear in his face, he shifted uncomfortably in his chair. When I finished my explanation, I could tell he was torn between the party line and trying to find a way to help me. To begin with, he took the first option, telling me that his company would never knowingly harbour or assist in anyone carrying out fraudulent activities. Again, came the robust vetting procedures before any tenancy agreement was offered. They had been trading for over twenty years and had other premises in the city and outside.

I assured him that I was not in any way, accusing or criticizing the company of any wrongdoing and had no intention undermining his position. At this point, I assured him I just needed to trace Gerard Reynolds. This seemed to change his perspective. He opened one of his cabinets and leafed through it and took out a file. He untied the string and set the contents on his desk. He had obviously remembered something as he searched through them.

'I cannot let you have copies of these.' He waved his hand over the papers.

'I know, Data Protection.'

'However, as this is in the public domain, so to speak, have a look.'

He handed me a Local Council bailiff's letter addressed to Gerard Reynold. I took out my pen and made some brief notes.

'We had no forwarding address, so it remained here.'

'Thank you, Mr. Evans. You've been more than kind.'

'Good luck.'

We shook hands and I left, phoning ahead to ensure that the signatory on the letter, a Mr. Freestone, Head of the Bailiff's Office at Wandsworth Council, was likely to be in his office later that day. I was sure to mention Gerard Reynold's name, hoping it may explain why I wanted to see him.

There was a smile on his face when I was ushered into his drab, file-ladened office brightly lit by several florescent ceiling lights.

'You're a lucky man.'

'How so?' as I took a seat opposite him.

'Well, he came to see me personally, in a rage That is how I remember him. See so many these days, but they are usually very contrite, wanting closure. Reynolds was not his real name. His birth name was Gerald not Gerard, and Plunkett not Reynolds. We have an address. Here.' He handed me a slip of paper.

'Did he pay up?'

'Not all, but after my guys visited him, we agreed a settlement and withdrew the Court case.'

'May I ask what else your guys discovered?'

'Seeing he owes you money, I'd be happy to co-operate, but you know the rules. I will be back in a moment. Please excuse me.' He swiveled the file towards me.

'I understand.'

He closed the door on me and left. I picked up their report and read quickly, making a few notes. Gerald Plunkett had been living at no.15

East Docks Road for years with his late mother, now alone he remained in the family house. University educated, bright guy. Spends a lot of the time in Spain, sunning himself, still a bachelor. I laid the file back on his desk just as the door opened slowly and stood up to shake his hand.

'OK, I have matters to attend to, if you'll excuse me, as he took his seat at his desk, then he looked up as I was leaving.

'Piece of advice, watch him, he's a slippery character behind the charming façade.' He picked up his coffee mug from the desk.

'Thank you, I've been warned.'

I was buoyed by how successful the day had been as I turned the key and called to Annie. She bustled out of the kitchen and gave me a hug.

'You're looking pleased with yourself. Tell me all.'

The next day I made my way by the Docks Light Railway to Canary Wharf, pleased not to be carrying an umbrella as I exited the complex of retail shops out into the bright sunshine. I walked south towards the Thames. I found East Docks Road easily and stopped outside number 15. I opened the latch gate and closed it behind me and walked to the front door and lifted the tarnished front door knocker.

'You'll not find Gerald in,' came a voice over the hedge next door. 'Gone to Spain for a few months. Won't be back for a while. Doesn't spend much time here with his mother's passing last year.'

'That's a shame, not seen him since her funeral, grand affair,' I lied. I worried that statements like that were coming to easily. I admonished myself silently, then continued, 'Do know where in Spain?'

'So it was, didn't recognise you.' He moved inside his house and fetched his mail from the hall stand and returned shuffling through the envelopes until he found the note with an address.

'No. Had a beard then and glasses. Contact lenses now, much better, but I recognized you.' I hesitated, trying to read his unopened mail upside down. He saw me thinking. 'Stephen isn't it?'

'Good memory. Here it is.' He read out and I noted it down. We shook hands and I left.

Two days later, on a single ticket, I was trying to get comfortable in row 14 of a budget flight to Malaga wedged between two overweight middle-aged women both plastered with cheap perfume that on one side failed to cover the stale sweat she was carrying. Thankfully, it was a short flight and breathing the warm air as I descended onto the tarmac, I recovered quickly, picked up the rental and was heading south on the autopista to Benalmadena Costa. I checked into the Palma Sol apartments a few hundred meters from the marina.

Next morning saw me strolling along the promenade and settling for a coffee under the awning of the Café Goya bedecked with prints of the famous painter, The Black Duchess, The Parasol, La Leocadia, I recognized, but the others escaped my naming them from memory. I felt very relaxed under the morning sun idly watching this world of colour pass by. The yachts, as far as the eye could see, rocked and glistened at their moorings to the sound of lapping water. They all seemed much bigger and more luxurious since the last time Annie and I had come thirty years ago.

Spain had become a preferred refuge for the dirty monied with a new passport and fun in the sun to spend their ill-gotten gains, but by now some had moved on to newer pastures. In one case, I thought to myself, he had left it too late.

After a walk amongst them, I stopped for a light lunch and went back to the apartment. I perused the list of items that I needed for my plan to work, assuming Gerald Plunkett, alias Gerard Reynolds, was still here. I had already purchased in London, the castor oil beans, which I now opened onto the kitchen worktop. I admired their beauty. Deep honey brown in colour, mottled with black dots. I discarded the instructions for propagation and carefully tipped a small number into my English saucepan avoiding contact with them. I only needed a small amount of ethanol alcohol which I carried in two small see-through plastic bottles. It was easy to obtain being used in the making of beer, wine and brandy, I'd taken the chance of bringing them in my overnight bag. I lifted the pan lid and poured the contents of both bottles over the beans, leaving it to break down the oils and fat. I had no real idea how long this process would take and so spent the afternoon lifting the pan lid to inspect progress. All I knew was that the murky solution should eventually become a clear light brown liquid. With each pan lid lift, I could see it was working.

I felt like a Victorian scientist dabbling with the unknown. My idea came, when I remembered reading about a Bulgarian dissident writer, Georgi Markov, who had escaped from the tyranny of Soviet rule in his own country. His death, from an umbrella stab on a crowded London street, had caused quite a sensation on 11 September 1978.

In the subsequent trial of his killer, Kamel Bourgass, an unidentified expert witness from the Government's Chemical and Biological Defence Establishment at Porton Down in Wiltshire giving evidence, revealed that the base of the toxin analysed was found to be a crude but effective liquid based on my beautiful little beans.

I had no intention of converting my umbrella into a pellet gun although there was a sort of romance about the whole episode of spy elimination.

The following morning in my kitchen laboratory. I lifted the lid off the pan for the final time. The castor oil had risen and floated on the surface. Armed with a garden mask from home, covering my nose and mouth, I slipped on my plastic gloves and poured the liquid though a coffee filter, watching the drips slowly fill my container. I could relax now. I hung the "Do Not Disturb" notice on the hotel apartment door and slipped out unnoticed into the noonday sun of the Costa del Sol. I was going to undertake a careful surveillance of Gerald Plunkett's home.

I had an address, vague description of him from Mr Freestone, but no idea of his lifestyle in the sun. I was looking for a short stocky man with receding blond hair with greying around the edges. I started to walk along the Paseo Maritimo towards Playa de Santa Ana. I stopped at the Palm 5 Beach Bar and ordered an iced coffee and unfurled my tourist map. My table gave me a view out to sea but more importantly an uninterrupted inland vista. I scanned the hillside that was littered with modern apartments stepped into the slope, wondering from a distance which one was occupied by Gerald Plunkett.

I left some Euros in the table and walked up the hillside, consulting the street map as I went. Soon I approached Calle Roberto Grande. Unlike those that I had already passed, these apartments had an air of opulence and superiority. So, this is where his fraudulent gains were invested. It would certainly cost very much more than the money I had lost. I was undoubtedly one of many poor souls. I approached Valencia One and looked up. Three apartments with unparalleled views out to sea with private balconies wrapped around each one allowing unlimited Mediterranean sun to warm the marble floor as it moved from East to West each day. Electric gates stood guard to one side of the half-stone wall with railing atop, behind which was the gentle sound of water dripping from the mature shrubs with yellows and reds against the brilliant white of each building. I was envious of the tranquillity and architectural beauty of the setting. It looked deserted. The quiet was interrupted by the distant bark of a dog. I lingered a moment or two longer, I was too conspicuous standing anywhere near Valencia One, so made my way back down to the shore, deciding to take a brandy at Café Goya hoping they'd know Plunkett.

'You have friends here?'

'Not really, just here for some relaxation.'

'You're from England, London?' I nodded. 'Not many here now, mostly Eastern Europeans, Russians, still a few from Scandinavia and Germany. You know senor Plunkett? He's English. Comes here. A regular. Very generous, senor Plunkett, he's from London too.'

'Donde puedo encontrarlo?' I uttered in my best Spanish.

The waiter beckoned me to stand, taking my arm. He pointed over to the Marina towards a grey-blue yacht that stood out amongst the white ones surrounding it.

'Ese es el señor Plunkett pequeño barco agradable,' he laughed. I was not sure exactly what he had said but I detected a little sarcasm in his voice. Later I would realize he said something about "little boat".

I finished my brandy and walked along the communal gangway towards Plunkett's yacht. Sitting atop the "Spirit of Gerald", I casually looked up and recognized him and wandered on looking at all the craft. He hadn't looked up from polishing a chrome rail, champagne flute in one hand, but as I walked back, he lifted his head and saw me glancing around and shouted down.

'Hi. You have one here?' His Cockney accent slightly bathed in middle English.

'No. just nosey. Taking some sun away from London. She's beautiful.' I added gesturing around his yacht.

'Not many of us down here these days, not like 70s and 80s. Come on up. Gin suit you?' he said looking to see if the sun was anywhere near the yardarm and smiling.

'That's very kind,' I said as I boarded the "Spirit of Gerald". He stuck out his hand and grasped mine as we introduced.

'Ice and lemon?'

We spent a pleasant evening together in which I divulged very little about myself save that I had retired early, but he, a lot about himself. He graduated with a science degree some years ago and was especially interested in the new burgeoning area of computers. He was a relaxed man with open charm, just as Freestone had described, but I remembered the warning throughout our evening together on his yacht. He generously ordered a taxi to take me back to my apartment. I had not conceived of another plan to casually meet again by the time sleep overtook me. I need not have worried as next morning, under my door was an envelope inviting me to supper at Valencia One with superfluous directions.

Gerald Plunkett was standing on his balcony as I walked along Calle Roberto Grande. I entered through the side gate and up the curving stairs to meet him. We sat outside savouring the champagne in the warm glow of the setting sun, nibbling corn sticks laced with red caviar. I turned the conversation to his knowledge of computers which subject he grasped with both hands and started to talk animatedly to me. I listened intently as he passed over banking security, email resilience against hacking or as he put, lack of it. One of his early appointments was as part of a team in a well-known international bank, testing their data security systems.

'Took me two days to breakdown their security walls, then another six months to patch over the cracks,' he said enthusiastically. 'Probably not perfect even now, but there are much easier ways to get money than trying to rob a bank or those who trust the system that is riddled with holes everywhere you look."

'What easier ways, Gerald?'

'When you get a reputation, others come calling through the net where I stay well hidden. Some pay well others not so, but the contacts are the things that matter. You know it was my first bank office job that alerted someone to seek my help not long ago. Cannot mention names but it involved a Government agency and international money laundering and assisting their operative on site. There I've said enough, just business.'

A thought crossed my mind. Penfold had rushed out of his office the day that I discovered the horrible truth of what he was up to. Could he have been meeting Gerald Plunkett. I put the thought out of my mind. I did not press him further, as I had a reasonably sound understanding now of his modus operandi, and how he had simply taken our money. As he was talking, I was furtively fingering the vial of liquid that was secreted in my blazer pocket, wondering if I would have the chance to use it this evening.

The opportunity came as I drained my glass and he rose to fetch another bottle from inside. I looked around noticing that no other properties appeared to be occupied and tipped a minute amount of the liquid, clear and tasteless, into his half-drained flute and shook it vigorously, probably much more than the 0.3mg required but it mixed immediately. I had learned all this from the evidence given in the Georgi Markov case. I inspected the flute to satisfy myself that it looked untainted, if a little darker than usual.

I stood and leaned against the railings looking out to sea, as he returned and offered me a refill and topped up his own glass. He started to reminisce about how he had come to Spain in the early 1970s buying plots of land and building cheap apartments, accumulating assets and then eventually settling here at Valencia One.

'Time for supper, Brian. Come on.'

Carrying our glasses, I took me on a tour of his home. It was elegantly furnished with rich tapestries, modern art and middle Eastern carpets and rugs. I had no intention of touching anything, until we passed one of the many bathrooms. I excused myself. He went to the kitchen, I, to wash my hands thoroughly, as I had been extremely conscious of the toxic contents of my blazer pocket and so far, I had not taken any chances of contamination.

During the light supper of gazpacho, sardine salad and orange sorbet, I watched him closely as we talked. There was expectation of vomiting, excruciating stomach pains and finally collapse but nothing seemed to be happening as my concern heightened. Had I failed to produce the same toxin that killed Georgi Markov? Two hours had passed. Nothing save he was drinking water at a heightened rate, dehydration. It was the first encouraging sign. He walked to the nearest armchair and sat down, I followed and sat opposite. Our conversation slowed as I watched him become listless. His blood pressure had started to fall, his head resting sideways on the cushion. He was now beyond help, according to my recollection of the doctor's evidence in the Markov trial. It was my turn to take control now I was certain that he would never recover. His eyes opened as I bent over him. He straightened his head and tried to focus on me, realizing that something was very wrong.

'What have you done to me?'

I started to tell him what he had done to my family and how I had traced his whereabouts.

'Nothing more than you deserve. At best you have three days lying here, at worse one day. Inside, your liver, spleen and kidneys are starting to fail as your miserable cheating life ebbs away.'

Without even a response, he slumped back with his eyes closed. I put on my plastic gloves, turned off the outside balcony lights, closed the heavy white calico curtains, cleared the table, popping his champagne flute into a plastic bag from the kitchen and into my pocket. For the next hour, I became a domestic cleaner, using the hoover, anti-bacterial wipes, bleach and finally wiping Plunkett's hands and face, he was already in a coma. I looked at him and the apartment, one last time and closed the outer door and left. I was satisfied that my efforts would stand up to the scrutiny of the Guardia Urbana as they messed up the crime scene before calling in their experts. It was unlikely that he would be discovered for several days.

It was now dark. The streetlamps were few and far between near Valencia One. I could not risk a taxi journey, so I took a long circuitous walk to my apartment shedding the wipes and plastic gloves in various bins well away from his residential area. The foyer of my apartment block was dim. The porter's shift had ended and with few others in the building, no night porter had been engaged. Inside, I carried out the same cleaning procedure, just in case anyone could trace my contact with Plunkett. I had already booked at flight out of Barcelona's Josep Tarradellas Airport. There was a nine-hour drive ahead of me with enough time for a detour to dispose of my saucepan and clothes deep enough in deserted hinterland. An hour from the airport, I had the car washed and valeted.

**

Mike was silent as Hillary finished reading her copy. Was this Roger Simmons' unknown man in Spain? He certainly lived the lifestyle that Roger had suggested. There was no mention directly of Penfold's case, but alarm bells were ringing in Mike's head, and they wouldn't go away.

'Another interesting MO? said Hillary.

Mike was silent.

'Are you listening?

'Yes. Sorry. I didn't mention it before, but I was thinking of going to Spain. Roger said something interesting this morning about using tech experts that worked outside the system in the dark web.'

'What? You are thinking this man was the one he was talking about?'

'Possibly. yes, I said that we needed to find him. I got the impression that Roger thought he may have gone rogue with Penfold's computer files, although he did not say anything. He was unusually silent for a time. You remember Simkins said something about Penfold leaving in a hurry the night he took a copy of Penfold's file. Well, a long shot but maybe that was this man, Gerald Plunkett.'

'You need to telephone him now,' said Hillary.

Mike picked up the phone and punched in Roger Simmons code.

'Roger. I think I may have found your computer guy.

'What! How?'

'His name was Gerald Plunkett, alias Gerard Reynolds. He's been murdered.' Mike gave Roger the barest details.

'Hang on a minute.'

Mike heard Roger's fingers on computer keyboard in the background as he waited.

'Yes, that man is dead. Seems the Guardia Civil has closed the file. The post-mortem was carried out in Malaga. The body remained undiscovered for over a week.'

'Were any tests carried out relating to poisoning? Asked Mike.

Why? Do you know something you are not telling me?'

'Can you tell me, please?' insisted Mike.

'The usual tissue toxicology revealed nothing, Michael. Cause of death suspected as a heart attack,' said Roger Simmons.

'Okay. Just wanted the details, Roger. There may be a link here between Plunkett and colleague Penfold and the missing flash drive is somewhere, either in Spain or here in the UK. I need to make some further enquiries. Speak later, Roger.'

Hillary had listened in from a distance, whilst surfing the net.

'Mike, I've found something.' Hillary read out; "At the present time, there are no specific clinically validated assays for detection ricin, the derivative of caster beans, that can be performed by a clinical laboratory". Clever man our Mr Simkins.

'He does his research and also anticipated that the body would not be found for days, making any evaluation of the cause of death or the timing difficult.

'Got away with another one and, just maybe, he has Penfold's missing flash drive,' said Hillary.

'That would figure. Tying up his only loose end so far.'

'He'd be a fool to keep it. Probably thrown it into the Mediterrean by now.'

Chapter 26

Some Time Ago - Detective Inspector Thornton

Session 9 Part 1

It was the eighth week since Consultant Raymond Childs had given Simkins the bad news. He had warned him that without chemotherapy his body would start to change more quickly. Despite not wanting to waste away, his daily routine of weighting myself had shown that so far, he had lost seven pounds or as his new scales indicated just over three kilos. He tried to combat this by eating little and often, but it was obvious that his digestive system was slowing down. Raymond had told him to drink fluids as much as possible. His dry mouth encouraged him to swill and swallow regularly anything from juices to gin and tonics. This week he felt particularly tired and unenthusiastic generally but preparing for his weekly session with Dr Carling forced his apathy into reverse.

Earlier that week, he had woken to a bright day and decided that he needed a change of scenery. He took the bus and walked down to the pier to his favourite seat to reflect and relax watching the ever-changing surface of the sea as it ebbed and flowed. That journey had taken more out of him than he realized.

As he entered the reception area of her offices, he felt himself breathing more heavily than he had noticed previously. In fact, just outside he had balanced his cane against the wall and lean against it to overcome the shortness of breath. Maybe he should take the bus back home this time, he concluded as he sat down heavily in the chair opposite her.

'Ah,' she said, looking at me, 'how was your week, Brian?'

'Getting noticeably nearer to the evergreen grass, Barbara.'

She laughed at his silly response. He was supposed to say, 'not too bad considering' or some such superficial garbage that was so understated. He sipped his tea and handed her his diary for this week's session. She immediately put them aside which prompted an anxious smile to cross his face which she ignored.

'After the previous session, as you were leaving, I mentioned that I wanted next time to discuss something that maybe important in understanding yourself.'

'Yes, I remember but you did not elaborate.'

'No, that was deliberate as I wanted to this session to be fresh, not rehearsed.'

'I see and what are we going to discuss?'

'The McDonald triad. You do know of it.?'

'Of course, I've been trying to figure out who I am for decades and read as much as I could on the multifarious theories propounded by police, psychiatrists, professors of this and that. Some helpful, others flawed, others despotically postulated until they are found to be impossible to use, like MacDonald. In any case when he announced his theory, when was it, 1963? I was already in my twenties, long passed being a likely candidate for his social experiment.'

'I see,' she said. 'That was not actually my point.'

'I know, you want to explore the basis of that man's theory in the "Threat to Kill".'

'Yes, do you mind if we do. It may help or it may not. Just another avenue to explore, so please bear with me.'

'Well, if you think there may be something to be gained, I am always willing to walk along the path,' I said with a hint of sarcasm.

'You have never mentioned Enuresis before?'

'Did I wet the bed? Why on earth should I?'

'Did you?'

'Don't all kids?'

'I'm asking about your experiences. As a matter of fact, Brian, no, not all kids."

'I'm sure that you have gathered that I was a sensitive child and as such was afraid of the dark.' She nodded. 'It was an unknown world, hidden from illumination and to step into it was full of foreboding and I suppose also the terror of what terrible event might befall me. Staying under the covers was protection, like being safe in the womb. Sometimes, I just could not wait for the light to come. Yes, I wet the bed. Nothing was ever said or talked about. It was if nothing had ever happened.'

'So, you were never rebuked?'

'No, the sheets were removed and the rubber undermat wiped down. It was not a pleasant experience for me to endure either. As I said, I was just another kid growing up.'

'Were you "just another kid"? I am uncertain about that. Can you say when this stopped?'

'Not exactly. I was always embarrassed for how long it continued. Desperate to go the bathroom, but unable to overcome the fear of the dark shadows that would take me to places I did not want to go, never to return. It was in these moments of fear that I would recall my father's disappearance or my grandfather's lifeless body. To answer your question, it was sometime during prep-school. It was a new environment that I had to come to terms with. In this sense it was a backward step for me for a while.'

'I see.' She could see that I was still self-conscious and upset even after the decades that had passed.

'Can we continue?' she finally asked after a long pause. I nodded, knowing what was coming and pre-empted her question.

'All children are curious about fire. Squirrelling away matches, watching paper turn black as it withers and falls. Watching the way different things burn, some slowly, others much more quickly, some producing little smoke, others more. It fascinated me. I was no different.'

'Is that all?'

I sat back, questioning myself. Did I deliberately destroy someone else's property, did I ever commit the act of arson as a youngster? I had never delved deep enough to answer that question in the past, but now I had to confront the possibility. I had destroyed Perkins' house. Was this the first time? Had I hidden something from myself?

Then it came to me. Barbara must have noticed me shift in my seat, as she leaned forward.

'Well?

'There was that nasty old man next door who had threatened to call the police when I had accidently broken the window of his shed whilst using a catapult with friends on a paper target in my garden. I remember we all ran away at the sound of breaking glass. I then remembered his shed had been destroyed sometime later by fire. Did I do that?

Dr Carling interrupted the silence.

'You know that unconscious fear-related memories can remain totally hidden from your conscious mind. We've also identified it as a neural defence mechanism designed to protect your psyche from being incapacitated by those panic memories.'

'Fear suppressed memory?'

'Just relax, Brian, and think back. Let me do my job. We have been doing well so far. I believe that you have more to tell me. It would be a pity to miss this opportunity to release the fear.'

'Was it a suppressed fear or just a lost memory? I do not normally forget bad experiences, even those of decades ago.'

There was a silent expectancy in the room. I looked at her momentarily then cast my eyes out of the window as if it was the seat at the end of the pier with the waves rhythmically rippling beneath my feet. She was watching intensely. It was raining, I would certainly take the bus home. I closed my eyes and there it was. It came flooding back as if a switch had been turned. Surprise and relief crossed my face in one.

'I was about six years old. Our neighbour's shed burned down. The smoke as it swirled upwards and then the flames that took hold. It became such a large fire, I was mesmerized. I remembered having to step away from the heat and run inside our house. 'I think I set fire to it, but I'm not sure.'

'Why would you think you did it?'

'I didn't like him. He'd been nasty to me.'

'Does taking the blame make you feel better now?'

‘Once I have rationalised the admission, I suppose it may do. I think it was the fear of being caught at the time made me repress the memory, but it was so long ago that I doubt it will make a significant impact on me now.’

‘I think you’re probably right, but it is an interesting revelation.’ At this point she took the sheets of paper from her desk and ticked a couple of boxes of the PTSD form, and then returned to face me.

‘Tell me about your relationship with animals.’

This was the last of the MacDonald triad, cruelty to animals. I considered carefully how to respond. So far, I was sure she was beginning to think that I would have been an ideal candidate for his social intrusion into my life as a child, to prevent me becoming a serial killer. What I was at pains to show was that ordinary kids with these three factors do develop subsequently into normal adults. I, being one of them.

‘I’m sorry to disappoint you but I consider myself the gentlest of people when it comes to animals. The only time I ever feel threatened is when I come across aggressive dogs with aggressive owners. I don’t blame the dog, only the owner.’

‘I see. That is good to hear. I don’t apologise for raising this theory, Brian. If we done it earlier, I don’t think you would have been receptive enough to consider the implications.’

'If you want my opinion, the theory was greatly flawed from the start, despite his concept being an urban legend.'

'I actually agree with you. All he is saying is that homicidal tendencies are linked to those childhood acts. Some say neglect, abuse and brutality. So far, our sessions have revealed some very unusual events and behaviour. I assume this another in your life?'

She held up my latest diary that flapped open in her hand.

'Look, Brian, let me be clear. I don't like the use of the words "homicidal tendencies" either, but I am still far from clear why you react in the way you have shown.'

'So, do I assume that you haven't dismissed in me, "homicidal tendencies"?' I said accusingly.

Dr Carling looked somewhat embarrassed but remained silent.

'You cannot conceivably come to the conclusion that I fit the triad or that am a serial killer who's never been caught. I think I made it quite clear why these people met their deaths at my hands. Each one has been justified by altruistic considerations remembering that others were to gain by their deaths'

I sat back, not realizing that I may have been intimidating her by moving so close as I let my indignation subside. I smiled a weak recognition that I should not have raised my voice or infringed her space.

'Maybe I have revealed, for the first time, something physical about me, that you had not seen before, only read about in these sessions. My obsession with fair play, justice, and what I alone considered ethical behaviour. I didn't really know, and you, I suspect are not about to tell me.'

Barbara Carling passed over the comment.

'Cricket?' she said leaning back lengthening the space between us.

'Yes, God's gift to the sporting world.'

'We'll see, I expect,' as she started to read.

**

I had known Albert for quite a few years. We had met through work. I had acted for him on minor legal matters on and off. Saturdays and Sundays had seen dressed in white flannels and usually several yellowing pullovers. Ah, for a prolonged spell of warm weather. Albert had been quite a good cricketer in the early days, but beer and work had taken its inevitable toll and now he had come to accept that his former glory days were gone except occasionally when he decided to concentrate harder than usual. I had always been an admirer of his ability but for those unfamiliar with the terms used in the game, I need make no apology. As a batsman, he seemed to have all the time in the world to assess length, line and speed of the ball and, most of the time, the position of the seam on the ball as it came towards him. He was always out to a "jaffa". At least that was his judgement as he made a hash of trying to hit the ball and missed. In all honesty, it probably was an exceptional delivery, but we all knew not to talk to him, particularly if he had scored less that fifty runs, until he re-emerged from the dressing room beer in hand. He was also very handy with ball in hand, left arm with a range of intimidating deliveries, bouncers, bodyline with apologies never sincere, accurate with the yorker. Then suddenly without warning he left, not a word. I did not see him again for several years.

One day, I recognized him lugging his cricket bag to the ground beside an old fading black car. Gone was the shining silver Mercedes of yesteryear.

'What brings you here, Albert?'

He smiled and we tentatively shook hands. The bonhomie had gone. Something had changed in our relationship, and I had no idea what had caused it.

'Ringer, my dear chap. Couldn't miss the opportunity to play against an old mate,' he said unconvincingly.

I looked closer at him. His hair had virtually all disappeared from the crown of his head and the edges were tinged with grey. His belly had grown larger, and his face was ruddy and slightly bloated.

'Played much recently?' I asked as we walked to the pavilion.

'Just enough to remember.'

'Work, OK?'

Albert Samuel Thornton was a policeman, the last time we played cricket together, acting Detective Inspector Thornton.

'Full DI now or higher these days?' I inquired.

No answer. I think he hoped I had not seen his face at that point. Anger and malevolence were the only descriptive words I could think of. Was it directed at me and if so, why? We had been good mates in the past. Perplexed, I walked on to my dressing room. Why was he reluctant to discuss the matter?

Having changed, I went to sit overlooking the green carpet of grass with the playing square beyond when Albert came and sat beside me. Surprised, I turned to face him.

'Come on, tell me, what's eating you?'

'Nothing mate, I was moved and appointed Head of the Cold Case Review Department. New offices in Kilburn.' He eyed me as I'd never been looked at before. A shiver went through my body, but I remained outwardly calm.

'Interesting?' I ventured.

'Very. Just me and a couple of wizz-kids and plods, when we need them, psychological profilers, and DNA. Don't need to use your gut instinct anymore.'

'Any tales out of school, Albert?'

'Oh yes, we'll have a beer after the game, after I've ruined your season,' he laughed and disappeared into the visitors' changing room.

I began to relax for the first time since our encounter. I hurried into our changing room to warn our bowlers not to under-estimate the red-faced, overweight little man that would probably bat number three. They apparently took no heed as Albert raced to fifty in no time at all. He was two runs short of a hundred when our captain told me to collect my helmet and shin pads and posted me very close to the bat.

Albert looked at me. 'Shouldn't stand there. You'll get killed with this crap bowling,' he warned.

'We'll see,' I said crouching down hands at the ready.

Groucho, our steel rimmed bespectacled moustacheod spin bowler, started his short run. I watched Albert's bat as he steadied himself. The ball hit an unusually rough patch and reared up, turning like a top. Albert stepped back slightly and aimed the shot directly at me. The ball hit my helmet and dropped like a stone onto my right boot and up into my waiting hands.

'Kill me, why would you want to do that, Albert,' I whispered in his ear as strode passed me. He stopped momentarily.

'Unfortunately, they've abolished hanging.' The look of bitterness on his face returned in that instant. We did not speak over tea.

His hostility became palpable when I came into bat at number 6. We were on our way to winning the match as I walked onto the square, I noticed Albert talking to their captain. He had not been asked to bowl yet, but that was to change very soon. As he was thrown the ball and paced out his run up, I sensed a challenge, a gauntlet being thrown down, a dual of hostility. I noticed, behind me, the wicket keeper and the two slip catchers move one pace to their right. Albert was expecting me to remain where it was, so with his back to me as he walked away to his bowling mark, I moved and took guard at off stump in the hope of combatting his left arm ball that would move across me from left to right. He had not noticed my change and I drove his first ball passed the beleaguered hand of the fielder in the covers for four.

'Lucky strike,' he mouthed to me and turned away.

The next delivery was dropped too short and rose towards my head, whistling past my visor and over the head of the wicketkeeper to the boundary.

'Any more of those and we'll win the match this over,' I pronounced with a smile on my face.

I let the next three balls pass by innocuously. I witnessed a sense of frustration as he turned away for the last ball of the over. His captain was in the process of ordering one of his fielders to change position, so I held my bat high until I was satisfied there were no other changes. In his irritation that things were not going his way, Albert had ignored what was going on and ran in, the ball rattled into my undefended stumps sending the bails high in the air. The umpire signaled "dead ball" as Albert screeched, 'got ya'.

I have to admit that I didn't help the situation by walking up to him and saying, 'have a little patience and play the game'. He kicked the ground and stormed back to his mark. For the second time in Albert's over, I grateful for my helmet. The ball was delivered with all the fury of the 1930s "body line" series in Australia. I tried to avoid a collision but was struck side on and I collapsed to the ground.

'Sorry, mate. Don't know what's got into him.'

'That was really vicious.'

I staggered to my feet, helped by two of the opposition and began to regain my sense of where I was. I noticed that Albert had collected his sweater and was walking away. The next over was a blur, but I began to appreciate that, Robin, at the other end had secured our victory as he took my arm and we walked to the pavilion and a trip to A&E. I was kept in for several hours as they assessed my concussion and eventually, I was released with three stitches in the cut by my left eye.

Sitting, waiting for the doctor, I had had time to reflect. I never noticed Albert collect his kit and disappear to his car. I was troubled, greatly unsettled by his actions. I had to find out more. What had happened to him?

Ron Edwards lived next door to us in Hampstead and had been a good friend and neighbour since Annie and I had moved in several years ago. Ron had taken early retirement from the Army. He had never talked about his career, but I assumed it was something special. I don't know why I made that assumption, it just seemed to fit. He was in his early fifties but looked years younger. I was happy to join him in the freedom that retirement gave us both. Our children were at University, so we also had that in common and as always over drinks, the cost of higher education loomed high on the agenda as with the inability of politicians to ever keep their word and the usual middle-class gripes.

A few days after that fateful weekend, we were sitting on his patio, talking, sipping a gin and tonic and watching the sun flickering through the leaves of the trees at the bottom of his garden when he turned to me.

'I hear you spent some time in hospital last weekend. Cricket, damn dangerous game if you ask me. You all right now?'

'Yes, they think so, so I must be.' I hesitated and he looked at me enquiringly.

'Actually, I want your advice.'

'Fire away.'

'It's about the injury I sustained.' I then told him the details of the day and Albert's behavior and our past friendship.

'That is worrying. Grievance, resentment, bitterness, ill-will, seem to have combined into something almost evil. Any ideas why?'

'I've not seen him for years until last weekend. Last time, we were best of friends playing our dangerous game of cricket. I just don't understand what could have happened.' Trying to entreat his help.

'I've never told you this before and you've been a good friend not to ask.' I wondered what was coming next, something special?

'My last posting was one I had hoped would never cross my path, but it did and now thankfully it will never do so again. I was ordered, well asked actually, to accompany a delegation to Kosovo just after UN had negotiated a ceasefire. You'll see why this is relevant to you as I continue.'

'The allegations that war crimes had been committed.' I interrupted.

'Yes, by the Serbs against the Bosnians. Some called it genocide. My role, as it has been for most of my Army career, is closely involved in the psychology of man's inhumanity to man. Ranging from minor grievances to major conflicts. One thing I have learned is that even the toughest soldiers can suffer from trauma.

'The point I'm trying to make is that your former friend has probably suffered some event that he has been unable to cope with and somehow blames you.'

'I have no idea, as I've said, what that could be.'

'I know somebody, do you want me to make some enquiries? In Kosovo, I worked with several members of the Counter-Terrorist division of the MET police in London during our informal sharing of information meetings. One guy, I trust, particularly springs to mind who I am happy ask to see if he can find the answers for you. Do you want me to make the call?'

'Of course, his was an unprovoked vicious attack. It was personal. He had chosen that game deliberately knowing I would be there. He set this up.'

'Leave it to me. Another?' I nodded and we sat in silence for a few moments, savouring the red sunset in the distance.

I said nothing to Annie, only that I was getting too old for live sport and that from now on as Ron had advised, I will become a spectator.

Several days later a plain no return address envelope was posted through my letterbox. I studied the postmark, Central London.

'Anything interesting?' shouted Annie from upstairs.

'No, just some bills to attend to, I'll be in my study.'

Inside, I closed the door gently and slit open the envelope and pulled out several pages of photocopies of an internal police review. It had not been redacted and was just headed "for your eyes only, destroy after reading" in someone's handwriting. Instructions to me I assumed. I began to read with mounting curiosity and a certain apprehension. It was headed "Detective Inspector Albert Samuel Thornton" and underneath the words "Competence Assessment".

The exact words I cannot recall as I did as instructed and destroyed the original, but the gist of the matter resolved around a secret obsession. I was not aware that he had been part of a team of officers that had investigated the disappearance of a Graham Parsons. There were various references to the events, the abuse of Sally Trimble and her daughter, Abbie and other assaults that Albert's team had concluded were committed by him before his disappearance.

So, I had been right in assuming that Sally and Abbie had not been Parsons' first victims. His predatory practices had occurred several times beforehand. I felt relieved and justified in my actions.

What came next was not so appealing. Despite the missing person's case being down-graded, Albert had taken it upon himself to continue pursuing the case and interviewed several of Parson's work colleagues after a note had been found, discarded amongst some seemly insignificant notes and papers in a drawer in his desk and not rigorously pursued by a junior member of the team. It read, "ST 3 Burl". Albert started to make enquiries but he was refused permission for a warrant to search no.3 Burlington Avenue as there was no evidence that Parson's had visited the premises on the night that he had been reported missing by his wife or at any time since, although Albert had known that he had visited Sally there, she had moved out to avoid seeing him again. The police concluded that nothing was to be gained by searching the premises.

Albert, without authority, had under the guise of an insurance value assessor persuaded the current occupiers to let inspect the inside. As a result, he had become obsessed with the provision of the radon sump and concluded, irrationally according to his superiors when they found out, that it may conceal something more bizarre. Also, his superiors gave no credence to the link between Parson's disappearance and the rehousing of Sally Trimble and ordered him to drop his one-man crusade or he'd find himself before the Disciplinary Board.

'At that last cricket match, he never admitted that he had been overlooked for promotion and moved sideways. He had apparently lied to me about the cold-case review appointment. He had been pursuing that neurosis, unauthorized and unsupervised, that led to him being given early retirement. Put out to grass at 51. There could only be one conclusion that I could offer myself. He had seen his downfall as my fault and was determined to seek justice in whatever form he thought fit. I reflected that he had somehow taken up my mantle and I was now the enemy. He had chosen the wrong adversary'

**.

Ex DI Albert Thornton read this session with mounting interest. This session was one that he would not be release to Mike Randell. It was too personal and would probably ruin his chances of their continued co-operation. Albert only wanted to extract revenge, not necessarily bringing Simkins to justice. He decided that he needed to meet Mike again.

Chapter 27

Present Day - Royal Oak London

Mike was ready for a long session with Albert when he arrived at lunchtime. As he sipped his beer, Albert appeared anxious to start the conversation.

'When Adrian Penfold died in the inferno at 33 Greenlip Road, as you know I was not the officer assigned to the case, but I had read the newspaper reports and noticed that the deceased worked for Simkins' law firm at the time of his death'

'Yes, Albert we have already covered that aspect.'

'Sorry, but I need to start way back, so you understand.'

'Okay, carry on.'

'Simkins is probably cursing himself for being letting down his trust guard that would normally be in place, but that was probably lowered by the alcohol. I think he had been too open during the time we had been close friends and talked about everything, but as always, he tried to protect himself by keeping a distance as he was very skilled at hiding his real self. Those diaries you have read confirm that. I was brought up in tough neighbourhood with uneducated parents struggling to make ends meet, they did encourage me and my sister to better ourselves. I remembered that he had talked about his struggles at school, the bullying, the death of his old Headmaster and his friend at University.'

'That is all documented in the diaries and confirmed by our joint enquiries, but there is nothing we can call into court yet, is there?

'Not yet, Mike but we will get there. Anyway, let me continue. We both had our quests for fairness and justice. I remembered one conversation when we had had a few after a match in the pub.

'That's why you're a lawyer and I'm a policeman, together we try to do some good. Sometimes, we fail.'

'True,but justice must somehow come to the rescue.' His exact words, Mike.'

'They added to my later obsession that somehow, he was a Jekyll and Hyde character. As yet he has no idea how close we are to nailing him one way or another. Mike.'

Mike sipped his beer contemplating what Albert had been saying, wondering whether this was getting far too personal between the two of them and why now a subtle change of urgency. He looked into Albert's eyes and said with a smile.

'Albert, have you considered that you may be next in line as one of his victims?'

'Why would that be? He hasn't a clue that we are on to him.'

'Have you ever, shown any of your feelings of animosity towards him,' asked Mike watching Albert's expression closely.

Albert laughed unconvincingly, nervously cradling his beer.

**

Mike sat down with a strong black coffee.

'Well, anything new from Albert. He's has gone very quiet recently. I cannot imagine Simkins has not had at least one if not two sessions with his psychotherapist in the last week,' said Hillary.

'Maybe he is suffering too much at the moment.' Mike paused, something was bothering him about Albert at the last meeting.

'Mike, what is it? Tell me.'

'Not sure exactly, but when I suggested he may be the next victim, he just laughed. Not at the absurdity of the suggestion. There was something else. It was as if he already thought that was a probability and he had a plan.'

'You need to put something in hand. Get the two of them together. We will know then for sure that the murders were premeditated and actually carried out by Simkins in such a way that we can bring him to justice despite his age and illness.'

Just as Mike was going to respond his computer lit up with a new message from Albert.

'I'm going away for a few days. Speak when I get back. Attached is some more background on Simkins. Did not pass it on when it arrived and forgot about it until I was clearing my desk yesterday after our meeting.'

Mike was unconvinced by the excuse. It certainly didn't sit well with Albert's avowed determination to bring Simkins to justice, nor did it follow the usual pattern of immediate sharing of the sessions. However, Mike and Hillary started to read the latest diary.

Chapter 28

Session 10 Part I- The Day My Life Fell Apart - 3 April

'Took the bus today.'

'I thought you looked better?'

'Better? Actually, I do feel more alive now that I'm here.'

'Bad week then? Tea?'

'That would be good. I haven't resorted to intravenous top ups yet.'

She had obviously noted that I wasn't out of breath like the last time, it wasn't my way to tell all. I was sleeping with pillows under my head and behind my back to assist in breathing at night or that the bedroom fan whirred all night.

She placed the cup in front of me as close as she could. I slowly stretched forward for the handle and cradled the cup in hand hands. They quivered slightly. I knew she was watching me carefully. The warm liquid slid down my throat and I started visibly to relax. I pulled my cuffs down hiding the reddened areas that I had been scratching. She had seen them, so I felt obliged to say something.

'My skin is quite fragile. A combination of losing weight, eating and drinking less. Despite the lotion, it is sometimes impossible not to scratch an itch.' She laughed recognizing that therein lies an impossibility.

Dr Carling put my diary down that I handed her and looked at her scribbled note at the start of this new session.

'Thinking back to last time,' she began. 'Do you trust me or are you still hiding at a distance?'

'Not sure, maybe I am still hiding, keeping a distance when we talk, but not when I am writing as you've probably recognized from reading my diaries. They are more open because I am talking to myself when I am writing. Do I trust you, more than anyone else? Yes, you have allowed that. The early years are full of examples of lack of trust and hence my ability to automatically distance myself from people and my actions.'

'Tell me about those you have trusted unreservedly.'

'Only those who have shown unconditional love for me.' I stopped short of putting names to those people.

'Aren't you going to tell me who they are?'

'I could and I probably should but my perception and classification of them changes as we talk and as I write. Most are dead now save my children. Perhaps I'll have the definitive answer moments before my demise?'

As I looked at her, a strange feeling passed through me. Were the dynamics of our sessions changing? Were her original inclinations of sympathy and concern for my situation changing now that she had been indulged by my confessions? All she said was, 'Perhaps you will. Anyway, back to business.'

**

I will never forget the events of the 3 April as long as I live. It was a sunny day, quite warm for early April. The children were both living their own lives, no longer needing Annie and me. I had retired and glad of the rest. Annie still had her Charity commitments. I spent my days reading and messing about with artistic experiments and the aerobic exercise for the over 60s, gardening. We were both fit, walking and cycling, miles each week. We had both filled out a bit but nothing to worry our doctors. Just the two of us rattled around in a house too large for us, but we felt safe.

Things were changing outside, more and bigger cars, more cyclists, both vying for tarmac supremacy. There were many times we would dismount and walk around junctions.

I stood in the porch as Annie put on her luminescent helmet and walked down the drive into the road. We waved to each other. I settled into my favourite armchair, untopped a beer, to watch England's last Six Nations rugby match, the Grand Slam decider. Just after the final whistle guaranteed England's win, the front doorbell echoed around the house. On the doorstep were two uniformed policemen.

'May we come in, Sir.?'

The three of us made our way into the sitting room and I turned off the TV and sat to face them

'I am sorry to say there has been an incident.'

'What sort of incident?'

'One involving your wife.'

'Where is she? Is she hurt?'

'She's been taken to the Royal Free. Can you grab your coat? We'll take you there.'

During the journey, I discovered that she had been found lying by her bike. She was wearing a helmet when she left. They saw no helmet at the scene. She had been attacked and her bag was missing. She had been found by a dog-walker taking the short-cut to the Heath through a well-used narrow lane.

'How badly is she injured?'

'Sorry, Sir, we don't have that information.'

The journey had only taken fifteen minutes. I rushed into A&E and was ushered into a small room and waited on the edge of my seat for information, watching through the open door oblivious to the rushing activity in the corridor. Moments later, a doctor arrived, I stood to face him.

'I have to tell you that your wife is not well. She received several blows to the head and is currently in theatre. The prognosis is uncertain at the moment, but we'll know a lot more in an hour or so.'

'Will she live?' was all I could muster.

'We're doing our best, she in excellent hands.'

I rang the children from the foyer and explained all I knew.

'We're all on our way.'

All three of us hugged tightly. Three hours had passed since I had arrived. It seemed like days pacing the small room, leafing through the old dog-eared magazines where the words didn't connect, trying to make conversation. Eventually, we were led into a private area of the Intensive Care ward on the fourth floor. Annie was virtually unrecognizable, swathed in bandages, her bloodshot eyes, minor grazes to her face. She attempted a smile for all of us. I held her hand tenderly, trying to compose myself to give her strength, despite the frightful sight that lay propped up in front of me.

We stayed by her bedside until it was dark. She slept most of the time under the heavy cloud of sedatives as we talked quietly by her side. The children left promising to return the next morning as I settled into the high-backed armchair with a pillow to keep vigil that night. All I can remember of that night was the diffused lighting and the constant bleep of monitors and the quiet breathing of Annie next to me and turning over the Surgeon's words in my mind.

'We're happy so far, but she's very fragile. I do not want to frighten you, but there could be other complications. We hope not.'

I was woken by a gently hand resting on my arm.

‘Has she said anything about the attack,’ he whispered to me.

‘What? No, nothing. Who are you?’

‘DC Blake. If she does, we need to know pronto. You understand?’

‘Of course.’

With a cup of tea in hand, I watched the porters and the Consultant surgeon gently manoeuvre Annie’s trolley into the corridor for a brain scan.

‘We’ll know a lot more afterwards,’ he informed me with an air of confidence of a man who had done a good job yesterday.

Annie seemed much better when she returned. The night’s rest had revitalized her as she sat propped up by an over-abundance of crisp white pillows. She beckoned me closer. I turned my head sideways to her face to listen. Her voice was faint and gravelly from the operation tubing, I supposed.

‘I’ve seen him before. The man who attacked me.’

‘Are you sure?’ I said surprised that she could remember after so little time and so much trauma.

‘Definitely. Hangs around the Heath.’

‘What can you tell me, darling?’ I tightened my grip on her hand.

‘Young man, white, dark hair, about your height but not as fat!’

‘Fat?’

‘Well, you know what I mean. Guessing, early twenties.’

She gripped my hand tightly. ‘Find him, won’t you?

‘Yes, I will. I won’t let this happen to you, Annie without justice being served.”

‘I know, you’re a good man, really.’

She closed her eyes and drifted off to sleep from the effort. I stared at her, taking in what she had said. Had she ridden into my past, why else would she have added the word “really”. That word would remain in my mind forever, but now I had to decide exactly what and how much I was to tell the police.

Annie died two days later with us at her bedside. She just slipped into a sleep and the monitors told the story. They tried to revive her as we stood horrified watching the scene from a distance. Annie lingered in a catatonic state for another two hours. I was relieved that she probably knew nothing about this world during that time. Not something I would want any loved one to witness. Far better to slip away quietly in one’s own bed, not a hospital bed.

Days later we were advised that, despite the use of anticoagulants called heparins which have an immediate anti-clotting effect and are administered to patients who have undergone major surgery, in Annie’s case a blood clot had formed close to the trauma injury to her head and caused a massive stroke. Her death was now a murder enquiry.

We laid her ashes to rest along the shoreline of the Gower peninsula where she and I used to walk for miles along the coast after Robbie Grant's death. I sat on a sand dune looking out to sea with the children beside me remembering a wife and mother and her tragic end.

'What are you going to do now, Dad.'

I knew exactly what I was going to do. I was going to find her murderer and extract revenge. This time it was very personal.

'Collect my thoughts, clear up a few things, might think about moving, but clear my head, first.'

'You know we're here for you. Just call, even if it's to complain about the weather.'

Today was warm and sunny, but they knew I always complained about the grey overcast skies and even worse, the snow.

The journey back to London was a quiet, reflective one. End of an era. My mind, however, was engaged in planning.; one of revenge. The attacker had probably never intended to kill Annie at the outset, but why did he inflict several blows to her head. Had he realised that she knew who he was after the beginning of the assault and changed from a mugger to a killer. Annie had recognised him, so I convinced myself that he was too dangerous to be allowed to continue. "Find him", she had implored me and so I would.

The team investigating the murder had kept me informed of developments. There were a few witness statements, but they appeared to be conflicting. The assault weapon was never found. The Scenes of Crime Officer advised me that there were unidentified fibres on Annie's coat. No finger or footprints, the ground was tarmaced and dry, no traceable DNA, there would have been blood splatter, but until they had culprit, it was useless as there was no match on their existing database. Nothing that could lead them forward. Annie's description that I had revealed could identify thousands of men in North London alone.

I had time on my hands and the crime scene was not far away from our house and so I took my daily walk down the narrow lane and onto the Heath as part of my regular routine. The first time was very traumatic. How could someone attack a defenceless elderly lady and bludgeon her to death. I searched the scene imagining the brutality. No-one heard a scream. The first blow must have knocked her unconscious. She must have seen her attacker and ignored any thought of threat. "Hello" or smiled. I would never know.

My first task had been to buy a new computer, decent colour printer and high resolution zoom compact camera. I was sure these would help, but only time would tell. In any case, I liked the thought of becoming a proficient and hopefully an artistic photographer.

Each day that I walked the neighbourhood and the Heath, I found myself staring at young white males of my own height. Sometimes I felt uneasy and moved away quickly to avoid confrontation where I had been looking too long at one or other young man.

Over the weeks I became a regular lunchtime frequenter at the Red Lion, the Drawbridge, the Kings Arms and my favourite, the Robin Hood searching for my quarry, then an afternoon of scanning digital images that I had taken, concentrating on each face in turn. I chuckled at the thought of a knock on the door with my computer being taken away for analysis and the thought of prosecution despite deleting a day's work.

Annie had said she recognised him having seen him before. This purported to be more than once and loosely tied in with the established theory that you are far more likely to be attacked by someone you know rather than a stranger. Based on this proposition, I had concentrated my efforts on the supposition that he lived or worked in the Heath surroundings. It was essential for me to become anonymous. This, I hoped was achieved by sometimes using my bicycle, others dressed as an exhausted jogger and on sunny days appearing with glasses and briefcase, hat or no hat and so the weeks passed.

One night, I was looking at my diary, the entries and the dates, when it occurred to me that maybe I was looking for the wrong type of person, someone who either lived or worked permanently near the Heath. The attack took place near Easter, student holiday time. I had been searching during the months of May and June without any joy, but summer was approaching. I checked on-line for the average term times. It began to make sense. If I was right, that her attacker would only be in the area during holiday periods.

My contact at the murder squad, DI Ronson had telephone me to say that they had reluctantly decided to slim down the investigation as they had no new leads. There had been no reports of similar incidents that they could glean information from. The case wasn't closed, but to my mind they'd given up. I questioned whether I done the right thing in withholding vital evidence but, underneath it all, knew that Annie would have agreed with my decision. Seven years with good behaviour for murder was no substitute for taking a life.

The one thing that had surprised me was that her bag and helmet had never been recovered or any of the contents. I knew there was a wad of cash as her Bank statement subsequently revealed. Had her attacker the sense to dispose of the rest of the contents and the bag, miles away from where he lived. I convinced myself that this was the most likely explanation. DI Ronson had said early on that this incident had all the hallmarks of a druggy needing to fuel his habit and the attack had gone badly wrong. They were overwhelmed with illicit substance abuse cases and muggings.

I thought back to our days as students. The workload was sometimes overbearing, but alcohol seemed to be the main substance of choice. Nowadays the choice for college students was much more adventurous, marijuana, amphetamines, ecstasy and MDMA drugs. They were all readily available without prescription, but they cost money, Annie's money.

Despite my underlying devotion to finding her killer, my resolve was beginning to waiver after a summer with no progress. I began to feel helpless and overwhelmed with despair. I realised I was beginning to fall into depression, questioning my weakness, my worthiness in the task, my masculinity was failing. The energy level had fallen, my sleeping pattern disrupted. Eating became a nuisance. I did not walk in the same self-assured manner, I shuffled instead, wondering if I deserved to be alive. I needed help. I knew that, but I tried to mask the truth. The headaches were becoming more frequent. I found myself shouting at other drivers on the road, drinking too much to aid sleep at night that I knew would be unrestful. I tried not to bother the children as I felt I would snap out of it sooner or later until one Saturday night.

'You're drinking too much. You need to see a doctor. Look at the state of you. This place and the garden.' Finally, I had to face the truth before something dreadful happened. So, with a new mind set, within a few months, my life started to turn around. A pride in myself and my surrounding returned, and the rest followed suit.

**

'This isn't the first time that you have felt abandoned, is it?' said Dr Carling.

'You think my wife's death made that feeling resurface?'

'Undoubtedly, but this stage it triggered a very different response because you, in your own mind, saw failure. You did not successfully manage to banish the feelings this time which resulted in your own self-assessment floundering in the unknown. In a strange way, I believe you may have entered a new phase of understanding yourself and your place in life.'

'Are you telling me that for perhaps the first time, I was beginning to feel free of the baggage that I had been carrying along the road to now?'

'Free from, it's too early to say, but let's see.'

She turned the page.

**

I found that to focus on one important matter brought me back to reality, I was probably expecting too much, too soon, when I started my investigation into Annie's death. I had not failed Annie, I just had not found out who killed her, yet. First, I resolved to tell the children what I was doing. On our usual Saturday get together, whilst the grandchildren were playing on the swings outside, I told them everything that I knew or thought I knew about the events of the 3 April and that the police were downgrading their investigation. At first, they were furious that I had not mentioned what I was doing earlier. Eventually, they agreed that as long as I was careful and kept them informed, it was probably the only way forward.

'Now I'm better, I am still going to bring her attacker to justice for your mother's sake.' I never mentioned the word "revenge".

'Promise us, if you find anything important, you'll tell the police. You're not some sort of vigilante, Dad.'

'I promise.'

In this diary, I had deliberately avoided mentioning that Annie's attacker had a hair lip and therefore spoke with a lisp. I had never mentioned it to the police either. I wanted an edge to find him and my extract my own version of justice, not some feeble prison sentence. This was my only personal contact with him, and he did not know it. Still at large, thinking he was safe.

**

Dr Carling held my papers across her chest and sadly looked across the coffee table at me.

'So, you have never discovered her killer.'

I had only given her half the story, but I was not sure why. There was something I just could not put my finger on, so I lied big time.

'No. I'm still looking. My need for resolution remains undiminished. I've still got some energy left.'

'Yes, I get a sense you'll never give up, but have you reconciled yourself to the fact that you may never find this man.'

'No. I don't ever think that. The pain of her loss has gone but the need for justice remains as strong as ever.'

'Time has passed. Whoever you are trying to find may have changed physically.'

'I agree but I live in the hope that our paths will cross at some point and I'll know its him, but then…..'

Chapter 29

Present Day - London and Athens Greece

Roger Simmons grabbed the telephone as soon as he entered his office at MI6 Headquarters.

'Where are you, Mike, at the moment?'

'Athens, why?

'That is convenient. Last minute city break, I know you two like them. Got a pen handy. I have had a request from our Athens office. I want you to give them a visit and report back to me'

'What is the problem?'

'It seems we have a missing passenger from one of the Mediterranean cruise ships. Seems the passport office are having trouble identifying him. Right up your street after Cairo. Our man in Athens has all the details. His name is Andreas Styros. Been with us for years. He was stationed in Malta. Did some good work when they temporarily strayed into contact with the Libyan regime. Telephone him at the Embassy and he'll arrange all you need.'

Mike wrote down the private contact number for Styros.

Hillary had been listening.

'What does he want this time?'

‘Some British ID on a cruise ship missing person mix up.’

Mike made the call and agreed to meet Styros next morning to drive to Piraeus.

‘You can come, there some interesting historical places if you know where to look. It will only take an hour or so to get the details from the Port Authority Police, then we’ll be on our own again.’

‘I will think about it. There so much here I could visit here.’

Hillary kissed Mike and lay back on the bed closing her eyes.

‘Come on, the sun is shining, a walk will do you good.’

Hillary shrugged her shoulders and Mike admitted defeat.

‘Sure, after a short nap, Mike, then we go out on the town.’

‘Sounds good to me, you win. Move over, you cannot take over the whole bed.’

An hour later, arm in arm, Mike and Hillary strolled around Psiri and took in the street art in Aischylou Street. The aroma of coffee hung in the still late afternoon air.

‘Let’s sit a while, I fancy a freddo cappuccino?’

They sat watching the everyday side of Athens city life soaking up the last of the warm sun.

‘Come on, Hillary. I would like to revisit Mars Hill. See where I am going tomorrow. Feeling fit after that nap and freddo?’

'Hillary started to skip along the street. Mike caught up with her and whirled her around and then set her down ready to push her up the slope that would give then a 360 degree view of Athens, just as the ancients had millennia ago.

They rounded off the day at Ant and the Cricket restaurant. Although Mike wasn't a great lover of Greek wine, here was different, the wine list was generous and expressive.'

Hillary read out the description, 'richer white wine with peach, lime and orange blossom and lemon oil all tied together with a soft fruity finish.'

'I haven't a clue how someone could write that,' said Mike laughing at the absurdity of it. Nevertheless, he ordered a bottle of Malagousia from Northern Greece from the Ktima Gerovassiliou.'

Cooled and bucketed, the wine slipped down very nicely as they over-indulging themselves on saganaki, fried aubergine and calamari appetizers followed by chicken masticato.

**

The Athens sunshine warmed them as they walked across the short distance from the hotel to Styros's car in the adjoining street.

'Welcome to Athens, said Andreas bowing slightly as he took Hillary's hand. As they settled into the car Andreas started again. 'Piraeus, our chief seaport for Athens. It is located on the Saronic Gulf on the western coasts of the Aegean Sea and the largest port in Greece and one of the largest in Europe. We therefore have a large police presence there and that is why all the evidence of our missing passenger is held there.'

The journey south took twenty-five minutes to cover the twelve miles of good road but heavy with traffic. As they arrived outside the police headquarters, Mike handed Hillary the Greek handbook with the pages open on Piraeus.

'See you soon.'

Andreas bowed towards Hillary, then escorted Mike to the first floor office of Captain George Andrino, Head of Search and Rescue.

'Andreas, good to see you again.' He turned to Mike and held his hand firmly. 'Strange business, this one.'

'Sorry, Captain, I am unfamiliar with the details of your investigation.'

'Thought I would leave you to explain, George,' interrupted Andreas.

From a pile of folders on his desk, the Captain took the top one and spread the papers in front of Mike. He remained silent as Mike took each page in turn, reading the events that had taken place on boards the cruise ship between Santorini and Piraeus. He looked closely at the passport retrieved from the ship and the ID tag given to passengers on embarkation to be worn ashore on excursions to avoid endless customs delays.'

'They were in the man's cabin,' interrupted the Captain with other personal belongings, including this.' He bent down and retrieved a navy blue sweater and handed it to Mike, pulling back the collar to reveal indelible ink hand written numbers on a white tag sewn into the fabric.

'Tell me, Captain, did you find anything in the cabin safe?

'No. It was locked but when we opened it. It was empty.'

Mike said nothing.

'You want these?' asked Captain Andrino.

'Copies will be fine, thank you. I'll make enquiries once I am back in London and report back to you. Thank you for your co-operation, Captain.'

Hillary was waiting outside having taken Hop on Hop off bus on a whistle stop tour of the sights like the Temple of Zeus, National Gardens, and Archaeological Museum of Piraeus. Mike took her to one side and whispered, 'no questions,' putting his hand to his mouth so that Andreas would not hear.

**

Andreas dropped Hillary and Mike in Syntagma Square in the central Athens. They found a small café giving them a general view of the square. Hillary tried to educate Mike by reading from their guidebook "The square is named after the Constitution that Otto, the first King of Greece, was obliged to grant after a popular and military uprising on 3 September 1843. It is located in front of the 19th century Old

Royal Palace, housing the Greek Parliament since 1934."

'Mike, are you listening to this?'

Mike nodded as ordered coffees and a brandy for himself and then proceeded to explain the reason for silence following the visit to police headquarters.

As soon as Mike and Hillary arrive back from Athens, on Sunday evening, Mike telephoned Roger Simmons.

'Sorry to intrude on your Sunday but I need something urgently.'

'What is this about, Mike?

'Your missing person on that cruise is, rather, was my contact in the Penfold enquiry. I believe he was following a lead we had. I'll know more in the morning. Roger, I think he was another victim of our suspect.'

'Oh my God, Mike, I am sorry. What do you need?'

'One of our safe breakers and locksmith. I'll meet them tomorrow at 10 am.' Mike gave Roger the address.

Mike sat down opposite Hillary at the dining table, fingering the stem of his wineglass.

'Hillary, I think Albert confronted Simkins on that cruise. He wanted to get him alone. We discussed this scenario and were preparing to put a trap together. He jumped the gun. Why?'

'Do you think he had all he needed? The two of you put together quite a file on Simkins.'

'Certainly. We had all the evidence but most of it, the important bits, were inadmissible in a court of law.'

Hillary was silent for a moment or two. Mike watched her intently.

'Albert was doing all right for himself, wasn't he? Financially, I mean.'

'That was my impression. What are you suggesting? Albert did say that he was going away for a few days last time he communicated. You think he jumped the gun deliberately using all the additional information we had given him?'

'Yes, and what for? I know it is a huge leap in the dark, but blackmail, Mike. You and I helped him in getting confirmation of earlier events. He had a complete compilation of every session that Simkins had spent unburdening his life to Dr Carling. All the confessions in the diaries that he had handed to her in total confidence. the evidence that could put Simkins behind bars, albeit for whatever life he had left, but Simkins has children. What affect would their father's arrest for multiple murders have on them?'

'Not a scenario that had crossed my mind. It is plausible. Often wondered about his income sources. The cruise would not have been cheap. You suggesting a lump sum payment for keeping quiet? Simkins is well off.'

Mike sat back and took a generous mouthful of wine.

'Our man is bound to be back in the UK now. It's been a week since that cruise returned to London. He usually has one or two sessions a week.'

'So let us assume, there is at least one session sitting in Albert's home. That is why we need to get inside and take a look around,' said Mike.

'Do you think Albert and this Carling woman were a double act?'

Mike laughed. 'No way. Come on let's wrap this up.'

One more thing, Mike.'

'Yes.'

'How come Simkins was well enough to leave the country and cruise the Mediterranean. I think that is very strange. Don't you?'

'It occurred to me but maybe one last look at the world gave him strength.'

'No. He was too feeble for that. Something must have changed. We need to find out. You have the wherewithal.'

'What? Demand clinical notes?'

'Not without a court order.'

'Rubbish and you know it.'

Two hours later, after Roger Simmons's intervention, a dosier of Brian Simkins' clinical notes arrived by courier. Mike scanned the first few pages until his eye caught the words "spontaneous remission". He handed the page to Hillary.

'Seems he has been given a lifeline, albeit maybe only partial and temporary.'

'Explains the cruise though.'

Monday will reveal all when we get inside Albert's place, I suspect.'

Chapter 30

Session 10 Part II- D I Thornton

I stood on the balcony of my cabin leaning against the rail, far below I saw the family waving as they looked up. I lifted my arms above my head to catch their attention. They had seen me as we blew kisses to each other across the widening gap between the ship and the dockside. Two weeks at sea with nine ports of call. My family's birthday present.

'You need a change, Dad, some sea air to breathe new life into you. Do you good. Time to put matters in perspective.'

The house had been sold, and a new apartment purchased. I was still in London, this time overlooking the Heath. We had had a massive clear out of years of hoarding useless items serving only my memories, replacing fading furniture and starting anew.

'You've got years ahead of you now.'

As I sat with my coat firmly wrapped around me in the armchair on my outside balcony, gazing at the overcast sky as the beginnings of evening set in, the warm sweet brandy cradled in my hands, having added my customary sugar lump, I would have time to reflect over the days to come but, I needed to make a conscious effort to divert my energies elsewhere since the last encouraging scan and blood transfusions. I felt there was a future for me even if it was fragile. Below, the ship was passing acres of containers littering the industrial landscape, I watched as we slowly left them behind to be replaced by a morass of green fields and the open sea. The warmth of the Mediterranean sun beckoned as I looked at the pictures of the ancient civilisations on the itinerary.

I'd opted for several tours ashore, and the anticipation was palpable, I just couldn't wait. In those first few days I had discovered that most of my fellow passengers were of similar age and those of us stationed on the upper decks had preferential treatment and exclusive areas away from the remaining passengers. I became familiar with my surroundings not wanting to mingle too much and only venturing to the lower decks for the pre-arranged on land tours.

I was listening to our guide standing in the shade, most of my face hidden under my large brimmed white canvas hat, sunglasses blocking the glare of the midday sun that reflected off the whitewashed walls, as he talked about the Minoan civilisation in the ruins of Knossos. We were all staring at the fresco of the "leaping bull", remarkably vibrant still in shades of blue and brown. It was an exquisite piece of art depicting a man sitting upright on the bull's back with two women in white standing either side of the animal.

As our guide started to explain the catastrophic volcanic eruption on the island of Thera, miles to the north, and the ensuing tsunami that devastated Crete where I was now standing, I became distracted as I'd glimpsed a man walking towards the far side of our group, his head facing sideways away from me as he appeared to listen to what was being said.

He was a man I had known for many years. I ducked lower pulling my hat further over my eyes avoiding his presence. I studied his figure through the gap of my fellow passengers, there was no doubt it was former Detective Inspector Albert Samuel Thornton. "What the hell is this man doing here?" I said to myself. I watched him walk away. All the relaxation fell from me like a discarded bathrobe. The history lesson continued as a far-off echo as we made our way from one treasure to another. It was a pointless exercise trying to concentrate as I was continuously surveying my surroundings to ensure I remained out of sight. The rest of the day passed in a cloud of hidden emotions. The only one that kept resurfacing was revenge. He had tried to expose me and having failed, he had resolved to maim or kill me with a cricket ball, all those years ago.

As soon as we had re-embarked and I was safely in my cabin, I picked up the telephone and dialled Information.

‘I’m hoping to find a friend of mine, Albert Thornton. Saw him briefly at Knossos today on a tour.’

I sincerely hoped he was not on board the same ship as me, that I had made a mistake, but deep down that thought was overshadowed by a feeling of “this was meant to be”. It was my chance to understand what had led to his actions that day, years ago.

‘No, Sir. Nobody of that name.’

‘Sorry, my mistake.’

I replaced the receiver and poured myself a gin and tonic, plunging two cubes of ice into the glass, strode onto the balcony and sat heavily in my chair. I gazed at the azure sea, flecked with red, under the setting sun as we made our way to Thera and the port at Santorini, the birthplace of that dreadful volcanic explosion some 3600 years ago. There was nothing on my mind save that I was sure that the man I had seen in Knossos was Albert Thornton, all the goodwill that had preceded this voyage began to evaporate. Why was he travelling under an alias. I was on another mission.

**

When I wrote this passage in my diary, the words flowed like no others ever had. I remembered the start of the page, the finishing words of each page. It was uncanny how the events were crystal clear as I sped across each sentence. She looked at me.

'Are you OK today, Brian? You look as if you've just come from somewhere warm.'

'Surprisingly, I am, Barbara.'

'That's good news.'

'I've succumbed. After last week, I had delivered an oxygen tank and mask. The purity of those breaths seems to keep me going much longer as result, I'm sleeping much better.'

'You certainly seem livelier today.'

I refrained from telling her about my scan and the good news. I wanted her continued sympathy to remain high

'You've noticed that I don't moan and groan so much.' She laughed, so I continued.

'Actually, my pain levels got really bad after our last session that I had to do something about it. I am not one for taking drugs, but it became intolerable. Raymond put me on some high-octane painkillers which actually work. He said they were terribly additive, so I had to remind him of his diagnosis.'

She clearly wanted to ask me something and perhaps after discussing my ailments thought better of it.

'Go on, ask me the question, I'm fine,' I insisted. She hesitated a moment.

'Anger, that's what I want to talk about today. It is a very strong word, but throughout our sessions, I can see that, on occasions, that the anger you have, becomes hostility. What do you think?'

'I don't think I am an angry man by definition. Sometimes when I feel anger towards someone it can turn into hostility, but that feeling is usually enflamed by other factors. Isn't that a normal human reaction?'

So, you believe that you are Mr Average in this respect?'

'Yes.'

'I see, but don't you think that is being a bit too subjective. The memories that you have described to me as traumatic, may well be so, but as they are not always concerning issues against you, for example, Sally and Abbie. Here, you seem to make the anger, personal. Surely, we would all feel outrage in those circumstances, but then not make it our sole responsibility to extract justice. What you told me about your calculated reaction to each event appears to be unique to you, Brian.'

'You are telling me that my anger or rage shouldn't be my first reaction?'

'Exactly. Anger is normally a secondary emotion. Sadness or fear are usually the first.'

'Haven't we discussed my lack of fear? You said it could be linked to my concussions and that CAT scan result. Are you ignoring that? So, I'm not Mr Average?'

'It could be concluded that because of your fearlessness, that anger is your first emotion and that's not what most of us experience, so that's my conclusion. Your reactions are too intense to be classified as normal. Taking that further, I would also say that you are hyper-vigilant?'

'Not sure what you mean?'

'Well, do you constantly experience the necessity to be ready for any kind of threat? From what you written and told me, Brian, you seem to be in a constant state of sensory sensibility, increased anxiety, if you like. You spend a lot of time searching for sights and sounds of people's behaviour, anything that is reminiscent of threat or trauma that you've experienced.'

'You mean that I'm on high alert in an obsessive way?'

'Yes.'

'Do you mean now or in the past?'

'Both. Here, let me pour you another tea.'

I was silent for a while, supping the tea slowly, thinking. The non-average, so full of anger and hyper-vigilant This was a difficult one for me to answer, off the cuff. I travelled back, remembering the pain of my birth, the deaths I had encountered, the bullying, the abandonment, analysing the injustices of them all and how I had internalised them all and found my wonder drug which was setting those experiences so far to the back of my sub-consciousness that they were and are completely hidden from everyone including myself, but always…

'Yes, I was and still am hyper-vigilant,' I finally uttered. She stretched towards her desk with pen in hand and ticked two more PTSD boxes, then settled back to re-read the first few pages again in the light of our anger discussion, as I continued to sip my tea.

**

I had already booked a tour of the island of Santorini but decided to cancel it for fear that Albert might be amongst our group. The harbour at Skala Fira was too small and shallow, so our ship anchored offshore and tendered those wanting to visit into the island. I still made the trip ashore in the privileged position of being one of the first there. The little town of Thira the capital lies atop a thousand foot cliff that can only be reached by cable car, bus or donkeys that negotiate the winding footpath and steps. As I set foot on the harbour wall, I awaited, ignoring the bustle of touts selling their wares and offered inflated rates of transport around the island. I sank back into shadows and awaited. I wanted to be sure that I hadn't made an identity mistake. After about an hour, I spotted Albert's now rotund figure and bald head as he adjusted his sunhat. He did not hesitate once he had pushed his way through the surge of fellow passengers and made his way to a waiting bus. I saw his face looking my way, I was certain now, as I slid against the wall dropping from a standing position onto the dusty ground. He looked away uninterested.

As soon as his bus moved away, I made my way to the entrance of the cable car and settled in the first available seat. Soon with a jerk and a gentle sway, it glided upwards. The view into the caldera was spectacular. The basin was filled with deep blue water occasionally broken by the white wake of a speed boat. It took my breath away as we moved higher. Below, the parched landscape sped by until the car jerked below the last pylon and came to rest at the top station. I consulted my map and followed the signs to Central Square and the bus terminal through the gleaming white houses and villas topped with blue tiles, turning right at Martiou Street, I kept walking at a brisk pace, catching the shadows as much as I could. I had reached the flat part of town and stopped to wipe my brow and pulled my hat down repositioning by sunglasses. As I arrived in Central Square, the no.5 bus had already arrived and disgorged its curious disoriented passengers. There amongst them, I spotted Albert, folding his map. He strode off to his right, I assumed towards the Orthodox Cathedral on Papantis Street. I mingled with the gaggle of other tourists making their way in the same direction at a more sedate pace.

Until this morning, I had been unable to gauge the situation and had no real plan how to confront him, but that changed when I checked my on-board account earlier that morning. It was clear that his vehement resentment of me still existed. Now I knew three further things about him. Firstly, he was a dishonest fraud and a thief and secondly, I suspected, no, knew for certain that he had planned this trip with me in mind.

How had he known? Was I under surveillance? If so by what method? Thirdly, why he had needed to disguise his presence here on this ship. I needed time to think, now that I knew he had his eye on me since we sailed from London, but that meant that he had known long before. My children had booked months in advance. I had an uneasy feeling of being caught it a maze, not knowing which way to turn to find a way out. In the end, I concluded that it did not matter now. It was just him and me. I decided to leave him to his own devices and took a bus to the ruined village of Akrotiri to see the Minoan Bronze Age settlement that was buried in the volcanic ash of that explosion which had preserved the remains of fine frescoes and many objects and artworks, not as famous as those of Herculaneum or Pompeii, but nevertheless priceless.

I sat in a small taverna aside the ruins and took papers from my pocket and started to leaf through them.

Surprisingly, I felt elated as I pawed over the signed bar chits with my passable signature forged on each one. He must also have somehow realised that some bars were not usually frequented by top deck occupants, but the casino was and the bulk of what spread out in front of me were from there including some expensive snacks.

I ambled back to the bus stop, joining a small queue of tourists, for the journey back to Thira. There was no sign of Albert in town or on the cable car. I scanned those waiting for the tender and satisfied he was not there, boarded last.

Once in my cabin, I showered away the day's dust and sat on my balcony. Bit early for brandy, but what the hell. I had dressed down for the occasion and went to find and confront him.

After an hour of wandering around the many decks and restaurants, I found him lounging alone beside the pool at the stern watching the receding island as the ship gathered speed. He was nursing a large glass of amber liquid as I approached and drew up a chair in front of him.

'Hello, Albert. Did I pay for that?' I said pointing at the glass.

'Ah, you've found me at last. Knew you would not give up once you had seen me in Knossos. Of course, you paid, you can afford it.'

'So, can you. You're here aren't you. Who paid for your ticket?'

'Not sure.'

'What do you mean, not sure?'

'Since you dropped me in it and I was booted out of the force, I've developed some quite interesting sources of income.'

This, of course, was his neurosis. I had had nothing to do with his dismissal. It was his fixation on nailing me for crimes I had committed that he couldn't prove. I refrained from taking the bait.

'Care to tell me about it, apart from forgery, travelling on a fake passport and impersonation?'

'It's called "blackmail" and you're on my list. One good turn deserves another.'

A wave and two brandies arrived. He signed my name in front of me. He had certainly crossed from being good cop to bad cop.

'Why me, Albert?'

'You're the one whose complaint led to the internal enquiry that had me suspended.'

'Complaint about what?' I had no idea what he was referring to. I had made no complaint.

'Probing into your private life.'

'I did not complain to anyone. I didn't even know you were probing.'

'Liar.' His face was red with fury although he kept his voice steady. I looked around nervously to make sure no-one was watching us. The barman was far enough away not to hear and was engaged in cleaning the bar. No-one else was around, late dinner had been called, I assumed.

'There was a note on my file with you surname clearly visible. I saw it with my own eyes. No-one else knew that I had you in my sights. How else did it get there?' He fell silent.

'What else did you see, Albert?'

'The Internal Affairs investigation had me overstepping public personal boundaries, conducting police work in my own time, impersonation, wasting resources and re-opening closed cases.'

'So how did my name have significance, Albert?'

Another double brandy arrived as I listened to his meanderings through his extra-mural investigation.

'I have it all documented. Deliberately brought it with me to convince you that I am serious. Very precious. It is my bank account, one of many, I can tell you. The rest are secure at home, only yours with me, as I needed to ensure you read it and know the consequences of not co-operating.' He raised his glass and downed the double.

'Come on, keep up.' He beckoned the barman again then turned to me and mumbled under his breath just loud enough for me to hear.

'You're a murdering supercilious bastard, aren't you? Go on admit it. You killed those people. Your wife knew it.'

'*You're a good man really.*' Annie's last words to me echoed loudly in my head again.

'Met her one day, as I was returning from Perkins' ashes. Asked her a few pertinent questions about this and that including the house you sold in Burlington Avenue. Set her thinking, I guess particularly when I mentioned Robbie Grant. She looked uncomfortable, is what I'd say. Did she tell you we'd had a little chat?'

I turned away. She had never mentioned seeing Albert. '*You're a good man really*' now made complete sense for the first time.

'Didn't think so.'

Annie had been the one to contact Internal Affairs. He had accused the wrong person. She had protected me and our family. She had not known why I was driven to take these events in hand personally, but she may have understood my underlying motivation. I really hoped so. I comforted myself in those last words to me in hospital. '*You're a good man really*' echoed through my mind again.

'So, down to business. I have everything I need to nail you good and proper, and I will if we don't come to some amicable arrangement.' He was beginning to hesitate over the longer words, trying to arrange the letters in a comprehensible sequence that the brandies were impeding. I ordered two more just as the bar was closing, tossing my existing glass-full unobserved onto the deck and emptying most of the new one in the same way as I walked back. I returned and handed him the new glass.

'A lump sum would do me fine. A monthly stipend would be normal, but you don't have time, dear fellow. Do you? Shall we say fifty thousand?'

'And what if I say "no".'

'I give your dossier to my old mates and you'd be spending your last few months locked up for all to know including your dear children. I am sure you do not want that to happen.'

I ignored the threat and poured the remainder of my brandy into his glass and said I would sleep on it. I put my empty glass on the bar, bidding the barman a good evening and as I was in unfamiliar territory asked for the most direct route to my cabin flashing my pass and stifling a fake yawn. He pointed up the outside stairs to the Upper Deck. I looked back over my shoulder. Albert had slumped a little further in his chair. I faded into the shadows.

The ship was well clear of land on our way to Piraeus and the exploration of Athens, the calm waters of the caldera giving way to the gentle swell of the Mediterranean, with the pitch and roll unsteadying my feet as I waited. The minutes passed, finally the cooler air forced Albert to rise, clearly unsteady on his feet as he lurched towards the rail separating him from waters below, his other arm clutching the barman who opened the first of two doors leading into the cafeteria. I stood watching as he shook off the steadying hand of the barman who quickly locked up and turned off the lights, disappearing into the "crew only" entrance. I walked towards Albert as the second automatic door slid open. I had to get him outside again somehow. I needn't have worried, he had no idea where he was and fell against the metal rail and sank to his knees and onto the carpet. I pulled him upright.

'Come on, let me help you. Where is your cabin?'

He pointed to his pocket. I felt around and pulled out his plastic key card and put it in my trouser pocket.

'Hold onto to me. We don't want another fall, do we?'

I grasped his arms and steadied him against my shoulders, turned and made it through the first door again onto the open deck. The breeze had picked up and Albert realised where we were.

'Wrong way,' he blurted out, trying to pull away from me.

'No. you went through the wrong door. It's the one over here for your side of the ship.'

He relaxed a little as I tightened my grip, looking around I found that we were still alone. We stumbled across the open deck and again he slumped onto one of the chairs bringing me to my knees as I held on.

'Not far now and we'll be safe inside the warmth.'

I pulled him upright, looking around again. This time I was determined to make him move quickly. I tried to lift him off the deck managing only to drag him forcibly towards the other door as we approached, he looked up at me. It was then I hurriedly changed direction and pinioned him against the railing, the top part of his body balanced precariously as I lifted his feet high above his head. He let out a plaintiff cry for help as he disappeared into the darkness below. I hesitated then heard a faint splash in the breeze and then he was lost in the foam of the ship's wake. I cursed myself that he had taken my linen jacket with him as he clung to me, but it his last futile effort to save himself. Goodbye to my expensive sunglasses as well.

I looked at my watch, only a few hours to sunrise. Peering around each corner and taking the stairs, I made my way to his cabin. Everywhere was deserted. The gangways had long seen the passengers to bed, even the Casino lights were dimmed and the slot machines unlit, lying idle. Alberts's cabin was near the staircase I had taken. I looked around for the last time, pressed the plastic pass key into the door lock and slide into his cabin unobserved, I picked up a hand towel and reached around to place the "Do not Disturb" notice on the hook outside. With my feet in his slippers and towel in hand, I began my search. The wardrobes and drawers revealed nothing unusual. Hidden under his case and several pairs of underwear was the cabin's safe, opened by a security code of numbers. I pulled at the handle, it held fast, no movement. I looked at the time again, so far it had been fifteen minutes since Albert went swimming.

I placed a bath towel on the bed and sat down, looking around. I had replaced each item as I had found it, then I remembered the navy-blue polo-neck sweater, those issued to the police, that I'd seen in his wardrobe. Sitting back on the bed, I peeled back the collar and there written on the name tag was his police number. I tapped the figures into the safe keypad, there was a sound, I pulled down the handle and opened the door. Inside, there was only a tightly rolled sheaf of papers. A mere glance told me I had what I had come for. I closed and locked the safe and tucked the papers inside my shirt. Wiping down all surfaces that I might have touched and tidying the bed, I replaced the sign, tucked his slippers under my arm and closed the door slipping into my shoes.

Back in my cabin, I started to read the wealth of information he had about me. One question arose? How had he obtained detailed information of all my diaries to date. A complete compilation of every session that I had spent unburdening my life to Dr Carling. All the confessions in my diaries that I had handed her in total confidence. This was something that I was going to withhold from Barbara Carling because they were not acting together, not a double act. She never gave an inkling of recognition when his name was first mentioned. No, I trusted Dr Carling. How could he have done this? The first diary was there. He knew I was ill so he must have had me followed and realising that I had arranged to see a psychotherapist, had her offices put under extensive surveillance. It was his last chance to nail me. Further, of course, he was now not with us to take advantage of any further intrusion into her office or my life. I would skip this part of my confessions. Barbara Carling would never know about this part of Albert's work.

I sat on my bed, thinking what to do about the notes that lay around me. I ran a hot water bath and dropped each page into the hot water. It was a damning exhibition of ingenious detective work that he had dedicated himself to. I felt relief set in as I swirled the warm water watching it turning a shade of light grey as the ink lifted off the pages as I did so. I left them in the cooling water and caught a few hours sleep. I woke to the thought that Albert was a fine detective, much more accomplished than most of his colleagues. He had a nose and used it to great effect. I actually felt sorry that the police force didn't have enough resources to allocate time for the likes of Albert. His only way was to break the rules. If only he had the sense to channel his obsession more slowly and more discretely, he might still be with us, and I might be spending time at Her Majesty's pleasure.

I cleared the bath, squeezing the disintegrating paper into large balls and put them in my empty case until nightfall when I would toss them into the Mediterranean to be lost for ever. Rumours started to spread about someone being lost overboard and a search and rescue being launched from Athens. As soon as we had docked at Piraeus much earlier than scheduled, the local Hellenic Police swarmed aboard. It was soon established that only a handful of people were able to assist, and the rest were allowed to go ashore.

The barman was the last to see him alive. I had left and gone to my cabin some time beforehand. The barman confirmed that he assisted Albert through the door into the cafeteria.

They were told by both of us that he had consumed a considerable amount of brandy as had I supposedly.

They had found that his cabin had not been slept in. No body was recovered in the sea search. It would take twenty years before Albert Samuel Thornton was legally pronounced dead.

**

'This one is different, isn't it?' asked Dr Carling.

'In what way?'

'Well, I haven't seen you for some time, and you look and act differently. This event you've just described isn't historical. Is it?' In Dr Carling's mind the dynamics had now changed. She was careful not to show her concern. Opposite her sat a man who had days ago committed a planned murder, an act of revenge. What professional constraints now stood in her way? Should she report Brian Simkins to the authorities for what he had just admitted?

'Have I been wasting my time over the past few months?'

I was silent, gazing across the space between us, trying unsuccessfully gauge her change in mood.

'Not at all,' I finally said. 'You will recall one of my earlier diaries. The one about cricket. I had no idea that Albert Thornton had deliberately followed me onto the cruise ship. Nor did I know that he has been stalking me for months, years in fact. You know what I have written in those diaries.'

'Are you surprised at my actions, knowing all you learned about me?'

All the good of the last few weeks in remission seemed to have vanished in that moment. I felt exhausted and slumped back against the cushions and closed my eyes. Nothing was said, but I felt her stare across the table. I finally broke the silence.

'Maybe in the light of what I have already admitted to you in those papers.' I pointed the ever-increasing pile of diaries accumulating on the desk behind her.

'You have to remember to view all those in isolation,' I said pointing to her desk. 'Albert had no knowledge of the reasons, the motives, behind my actions. He only saw or thought he saw the aftermath, a serial killer despatching innocent people. He never considered any other point of view.

'He threatened me, cajoled my late wife, attempted blackmail, fraudulently stole my money and tried to maim or kill me on the cricket field.'

'Those previous actions were motivated by a sense of bringing in justice. That is what you said. Here, you were trying to protect yourself against exposure. You were not seeking justice, per se,' said Dr Carling raising her voice slightly.

'Chicken and egg.' I slumped back again. 'We won't agree on this one. I've said all I need to say.' I was breathing hard, trying to stay in control.

'Are you all right?'

I thought as she got up, she was going to put a hand on my shoulder, but no, something had now changed between us. I realised that this last confession had, perhaps, undermined her professional confidence in her quest to assist me in understanding myself and that all her perceptions and explanations were for nothing.

'Let me get you a taxi home.'

The next session I cancelled. I was too weak to even rise from my bed. That week, my headaches were more frequent and more severe. The weekly blood test showed a significant fall in my red blood cell count. Raymond Childs suggested another transfusion. I acceded and spent a day in hospital, watching the red liquid bags release their contents into my arm. A few days later, I felt much more alive. He had been right about that. I did not know it then but my re-arranged meeting with Dr Carling would be my last.

Chapter 31

Session 11- The Ending is Nigh

'Sorry about the last session I cancelled.' I didn't mention that Raymond Childs had been wrong about the possibility of a permanent remission.'

'No problem, Brian.'

I handed Dr Carling my last diary as I entered her consulting room.

'You are looking well today.'

'Blood transfusion. I have someone else's life running around inside me. More oxygen going where it should go. Probably someone young and vigorous.' I laughed. 'Sadly, I have to admit this maybe our last session.' She saw the pain of my life ebbing away.

'I shall miss these times, despite what I said and felt last time.'

'So, will I,' I admitted sadly. I took the cup of tea from her hands and sipped it gently. Swallowing these days was an effort. Each mouthful took several attempts. I noticed her watching me intently. She shook her head out of the stare.

'I thought, first of all, that we talk about PTSD. I completed the questionnaire and sent it to my colleague. Dr Pike has analysed the results and spoken at length to me. He and I believe that your very early experiences, those pre-natal memories that were not wiped out by new neurons being created as you grew, undoubtedly shaped the person you were to become. You seem to have spent a lot of your early life hiding, pretending to be someone you are really not, unsure where you fitted or how to react in a normal way to situations that confront you, your dreams, your constant references to deaths you encountered, being abandoned. However, although historical diagnoses are tricky, we, have come to the conclusion that you probably suffered from the Disorder and may still do.'

'So finally, as I near death's door, you are telling me that my life has been shaped by a quirk of neurological development.?'

'Not entirely, you had that problem compounded by other experiences, witnessing or being close the death of those close to you and the feeling of abandonment and just as importantly the early internal damage caused by the head traumas.'

'Are you saying that, if it had been a recognised malady in those early days, someone could have treated it and made me a different person?'

'Maybe with time, your view of the world around you could have been altered and these confessions,' She held up the several of my diaries, 'may not have been necessary because you would have been able to rationalise your feelings in a more objective fashion without the need to take matters into your own hands.' She emphasised the word "may".

I sat back encouraged, sensing for the first time, that at last I knew that nothing that had happened was really my fault. The blame lay elsewhere in other factors and events in my past.

'Shall we move on?'

I smiled.

'You lost your wife some time ago. You never talk much about it. Why?'

'I am about to,' I said pointing the diary in her direction. 'I think it will explain.'

'Why the title? Not like you to be so pessimistic.'

'It is not pessimism, just a conclusion.'

**

My children kept complaining that I should get out more, do some worthwhile work in the community. That is what I decided to do. Try to help others, now that my depression had lifted after failing to make any progress in finding Annie's killer.

I got off my backside and went to the local Library. Stationed in the foyer was a large noticeboard. I scanned through the advertisements for bridge clubs, fitness classes, well-being meditation as well as a group of charities wanting volunteers. There was a bewildering array of possibilities. MIND was the one that struck a chord at that time in my life, so I decided with the little knowledge I had, I could go out there and spread the word.

I attended several meetings as an observer at the local branch. One the third occasion, I was approached and asked if I was willing to walk the local streets delivering their new leaflet. Things sometimes happen by chance. Of course, I could, so at the end of the meeting I was allocated a few hundred envelopes and a street map. I knew the area, and these were high end earners who may be persuaded to give generously to the cause. Did they want me to personally speak to the occupants, only if you want to and have the time?

I waited until the weather forecast predicted good weather, after all it was the summer. Nobody wanted to open the door to a stranger when it was raining. I had not taken much notice of each occupier's name just the streets and the numbering. I picked up my two bags of envelopes and set off with the local map in hand. The first street was an uninteresting row of semi-detached Victoriana set back from the road by a line of poplars that were just beginning to show their golden leaves. Very few answered their doors to my knock as I made my way down one side and back up the other, curiously looking at the names as I posted the envelopes through the doors. It was not until I got to number 14 that anything interesting occurred.

I saw a face by the front window and stopped, envelope in hand in the porch. I was in two minds whether to press the bell and announce my presence in case the face had not noticed me walk to the porch. As I was about to, the front door opened. Standing in front of me as a young man, dark hair and about my height. He spoke softly but I recognised Annie's description immediately. Momentarily, I was shaken after the years of fruitless searching, I handed the envelope to him trying desperately to control my emotions. I had the presence of mind to ask his name, but it meant nothing to me and did not tally with the one on the envelope.

'Day off work,' I said casually.

'Home on leave.' There was the slight impediment in his delivery of the words.

I hesitated, studying his face closely before turning to continue my deliveries with my mind racing, not bothering on any of the remaining calls to arouse the occupants to my presence and then rushed home. The picture I had of him was of one lounging against his front door for support, eyes watery and blood-shot with large pupils reacting very slowly to the bright outdoor light within his smaller than usual head. Someone still using drugs, cocaine or amphetamines. I was almost certain he was responsible for Annie's death, every detail seemed to fit in those few moments, but the bright bicycle helmet hanging from the handlebars resting against the staircase, clinched it for me. It was Annie's expensive rather large one that could accommodate her ball of thick hair that she always tucked under it. I had often wondered why her murderer had taken it and now I could see why, it would have been a good fit.

**

I sat silently watching Dr Barbara Carling absorbing every word as she paced through the diary. Unusually in these sessions she would look up, make a comment, ask me a question or offer an explanation as to my behaviour. This time there was nothing. I continued to watch her carefully. There was a heightening tension in the way she turned the page and flattened it against the previous one. It was deliberate and seemed to me to be gripped with passion. I had no idea what was causing the change within her. I reconciled myself into believing that she was anxious for me to resolve the sadness of Annie's passing so I remained a watchful spectator as she read on.

**

By 10 pm that evening, I had formalised a plan that would start tomorrow. A casual follow-up with his neighbours might reveal something, so much earlier than I assumed he would see the light of day, I set off with my bike to the same street. I walked it slowly along the pavement and leaned it against a tree scanning around as I secured the padlock. There was no answer to my knocking from numbers 16 and 18 so I hurried past his house that seemed to be asleep. I did notice the front curtains downstairs were open but there was no sign of life.

At no.12, I pressed the bell and waited, adjusting my glasses and slightly tipping my cap forward. Just as I turned to leave, the front door opened slightly on a chain. An elderly face appeared.

'Sorry to bother you but I was trying to speak to the young man at number 14.'

'You won't have any luck at this time of day.'

'Oh, that's a shame. When do think is best?'

'Early afternoon or evening.'

'Where does he work?'

'He's a nice lad, helps me with the garden, getting a bit too much at my age. He is still at college, been there for years. Knows a lot about engines, fixed my mower last year. Birmingham, I think he said.'

After a few more pleasantries, I left, removing my glasses, adjusting my hat so I could see ahead, retrieved my bike and peddled home. It was a long shot, but my guesswork had the basis of reasonable assumption. I had concluded that he was an engineer of some sort, probably, in view of the length of time he had been at college, involved in research. I typed these into the Birmingham post-grad University sites. One was clearly more practical and industry based and I plumped for that institution hoping I wasn't wasting my time.

The next problem was overcoming Data Protection laws. A direct approach was out of the question. In the end, I decided to take a short holiday in Birmingham, but I had to wait until term started again. I became more anxious as the days slowly passed by until the day arrived and with my files in my suitcase, I slowly backed the car into the road and set off. During the journey, I had time to analyse the assumptions I had made that he lived near the University to have easy access for the long hours that engineering students put in compared with some other subjects, rode a bike to and from the campus and probably ate the subsidised canteen food. He did not look like a self-catering foodie to me. Those assumptions may give me a good start in finding him. Ask enough people and soon enough he would appear on the radar.

The Holiday Inn was far enough away from the centre of town but on several different bus routes from the outskirts converging on the city centre. I was on a cash only trip for the next few days. No point in leaving an unnecessary paper trail. On the first morning, I followed the signs to the Engineering Department, looking for more mature faces amongst the sea of students. I needed more details of where I might find him if he was no longer a student but a researcher as I had surmised from his age. I gave them his name and was directed to the most likely building where I could find him. I walked purposely across the open space surrounded by modern blocks on the inner-city campus littered with maturing trees and seating for hundreds, out across an adjoining street towards a Victorian red-brick building and entered the foyer and walked towards a large noticeboard. I studied the various pinned details of the departments and locations and there I saw his name with a string of academic letters behind it, but no official title attached. No wonder I could not find him in the University's list of staff or researchers that I studied before giving up that line of enquiry and journeying here. So much for data protection. A sensible telephone call would have saved my time but revealed nothing. Two-hour drive, a bus journey and a short walk had revealed everything I needed to know about him.

I went to the cafeteria and sat with a black coffee dropping in two sugars and stirred it vigorously. Inside my briefcase, I had stowed a new hat, a rather bulbous dark grey affair but it did deflect from my whitening hair at the edges, and my trusty glasses. They impaired my long vision slightly but changed the dynamics of my face. Time passed slowly and the taste of the coffee eventually forced me to think about leaving, I was just about to get up, when he entered and looked around. Not a flicker of recognition passed over his face, and why should it, when we last met on his doorstep, he was spaced out.

I watched him as he ate a sandwich and talked to the others at the table. He eventually got up the leave, so I followed him to the bike park, donning Annie's fluorescent yellow helmet and then onto the road. It was long and straight with cars parked on either side leaving a dangerously small gap for two cars to pass each other in the middle. I watched him disappear into the distance and turn left at the end.

There were still many hours left in the day, so I decided to plan tomorrow as I sat overlooking the Grand Union canal, picking at a plate of nachos covered with chilli beans and cheese.

Next day, I drove into town and after circling around several times managed to find the perfect spot on the road that he had cycled down yesterday. I was anticipating a long wait and had to duck down as I saw him coming towards me after his trip home. He passed a car's width from me peddling fast as if he was late for the afternoon in his research lab. I watched in my side mirror as he disappeared from view, wondering how long I'd have to wait for his return journey. As it was a weekday, I expected it not to be too late but hoped it would be going dark. It did not matter for I had brought sandwiches, cold coffee, and my kindle. He still had not appeared by seven. As I started to stuff the empty cans of coffee and sandwich packets into a plastic bag, I started the engine and reversed into part of the now vacant space behind me to give me enough room to avoid having to manoeuvre back and forth if I needed to leave in a hurry. As I did so, I noticed the bobbling light of a bicycle at the far end of the road and the fluorescent yellow helmet gleaming under the streetlights that were beginning to glow. A closer look confirmed his riding style from yesterday, hunched over the handlebars with his head tucked in as you would expect in a velodrome race. I was ready with my foot hovering over the accelerator. Just as my plan was about to start, I glimpsed a car turning into the road accelerating towards me and him. This was better than I had ever planned, the timing looked more perfect than I could have hatched. So much for trying to eliminate chance. Chance had made my task easier.

Quietly, I counted the seconds, eyeing both the car and the bicycle. I checked that my car lights were off. As the oncoming car neared me, I started to pull out in front of his bicycle and momentarily stopped, his natural reaction pulled him into the path of oncoming car that had no chance of avoiding him. He tried to pull to his left, but the bike fell into the road with him trapped. I heard the bang and screeching of brakes as he slithered underneath the car, that bounced over him taking his life away in a moment. I accelerated away and turned left at the top of the road into the evening traffic, putting on the lights and making my way south east along the M6 then the M1.

His death was reported in the Birmingham Gazette the next day. I was interested to learned much later that at the Inquest, the toxicology report confirmed that he was twice the legal alcohol limit and that there were high traces of amphetamines in his blood count, accidental death.

**

I had noticed Dr Carling becoming more agitated as she scanned the last page of my diary. She finally closed the cover. I noticed beads of perspiration appeared on her forehead as she leaned towards me. I arched backwards slightly out of respect for the space between us.

'Accidental death!' she suddenly shouted at me. I reeled further backwards in my seat, shocked by her outburst.

She shot out of her chair and grabbed a picture frame from her desk and slammed it into my hand. At that moment, I realised what had been nagging at the back of my mind. Now I had the second chance to look at the photograph that I had briefly glanced at when we first met for my first session in her consulting rooms.

'Look at him,' she demanded.

I need not have, I now knew.

'You killed my son.'

Chapter 32

Mike's Apartment London

After an hour in Albert Thornton's house following Roger Simmons' permission, all written records, files, computers, voice recorder, printer and remote surveillance equipment were on their way to Mike's own apartment to analyse what exactly had taken place and fill in the gaps, of which there were many. The last thing put in place was the transfer of Albert's telephone number.

Once the tech boys from MI6 had set the equipment up and Mike had searched through the existing paperwork that Albert had supplied, the first surprise came when Mike and Hillary came across the undisclosed Session 9 Part I when Simkins set out the events of the cricket match and Albert's strange behaviour towards him.

'Looks like we are beginning to see Albert's obsession in a different light,' said Hillary.

'Did he really try to kill or maim Simkins?'

'His neighbour thought the incident was serious enough to help Simkins out.'

'That is true. So did his team-mates,' said Mike, 'but did it also put Simkins into one of his revenge moods?'

'I don't see why it should at that point.'

“I agree. He probably just wanted to make sense of what had happened, but it probably did make him wary of Albert after he found out that Albert was not a policeman anymore and that he had been dismissed from the force.’

‘Simkins probably concluded that Albert wasn’t a risk worth fretting over.’

‘Albert did not take your warning seriously. The one about him being the next victim.’

‘Did you notice the heading, Hillary?’

Hillary looked again at the beginning of the copy of the computer print-out of Simkins’ diary.

‘See. Part 1. Come on let’s find the other one.’

‘Here we are. I will print two copies,’ said Mike. After a few minutes reading, they looked at each other

‘Well, I can see why the Greeks dismissed it as an unfortunate accident. All the evidence points that way.’

‘Simkins unusual Modus Operandi. Clever bastard. We are never going to prove anything, are we?’

‘No. We have motive and opportunity. They were both on board that ship. They were seen talking together for some time.

‘I need to speak to Roger; we need to get this guy in our office and soon.’

Mike left Hillary having arranged to see Roger Simmons at MI6 headquarters. He took all the typed material that they had studied with Albert and all the Sessions notes to date from Dr

Carling's office. Just as Mike was disappearing out into the lobby, Hillary shouted after him that Albert's voice recorder had started to register a new conversation. She listened intently to first part of the conversation between Simkins and Carling. She realised that they would have to wait until tomorrow for Albert's man to provide the photographic copy of the actual diary. Mike had made it very plain that despite the raid of Albert's premises, all things should remain as they were. Hillary relaxed into the chair, thinking of the strange title "*The Ending is Nigh*", and Simkins reply, "*Not pessimism, just a conclusion*". Unusually, there was little conversation in this Session compared with others that Albert had transcribed previously. Hillary was shocked at the last sentence shouted by Dr Carling. Within seconds she was speed dialling Mike's mobile. It was message mode.

'Mike. Simkins killed Carling's son.'

She grabbed the tape from the recorder, her coat and hailed a taxi.

**

Roger Simmons and Mike were seated together as Hillary was escorted into Roger's fifth floor office. The table was covered with papers. She handed the tape to Mike and Roger and slumped down in her seat.

'Skip the first part. Listen to the ending, then you see why I rushed here. We could stop whatever is happening now. It is current. Going on now at her offices or at least,' Hillary looked at her watch, 'half an hour ago.'

Grabbing his phone, Roger Simmons shouted into it. 'Get the local mob too.' He read out Carling's consulting room address. 'Come on, we'll take my car. It has all the nobs and lights.'

With siren blaring, lights flashing they sped effortlessly north despite the deluge of rain bouncing onto the screen.

'Thank the Lord for bus lanes. Shouldn't take us too much longer.'

Chapter 33

Dr Carling's Consulting Rooms

I rose slowly never taking my eyes of Dr Barbara Carling looking down at her hunched over her seat. I placed the portrait of her son on the coffee table. She looked up at me. I could see the hatred in her eyes.

'I don't care that you're ill or that you are old, I'm going to bring you to justice.'

'And how do you propose to do that. Your beloved drug-ridden son murdered my wife for a few hundred pounds. Ever heard of the defence of Justification. I did nothing wrong. What I did vindicated a right of such importance that it outweighs the wrongfulness of the crime. An eye for an eye, tooth for a tooth and, in any case, I can now refer to your PTSD diagnosis and the events that cause it. That always goes down well with a jury of my peers, especially when I am wheeled in with an oxygen mask to plead "not guilty".

'You're still a dangerous man. I do not need a prosecution or the sympathy of a jury, I have all I need here. Her arm extended backwards towards her desk as she swept my diaries onto the floor in disgust, gabbing one and throwing it at me.'

I ducked out of its trajectory and stood, clasping my hands behind my back in a conciliatory pose and stared at her.

'It would be unwise of you to make an enemy out of me, even now, Dr Carling.'

I picked up my raincoat and walking stick and slowly made my way to the door. I looked back at her as she gathered together my diaries from the floor and put them on her desk. I sat in the reception area on the ground floor to gather my thoughts. The porter looked at me questioningly.

''Bad day,' was all I said.

'Tell me about it,' he replied gesturing to the pouring rain outside.

After that disconcerting last session with Dr Carling, I reflected on what I left unsaid. I should have told her that I was seeking closure. Honouring my pledge to Annie. Doing what I thought was right. I had no idea at the time the drug addict was her son. He was obviously someone's child.

I should have told her that he carried out a vicious attack on an innocent elderly lady that killed her. He was a murderer, but I did not. I just walked out of her consulting room unable to retaliate. However, by now, I had made up my mind. I rang her office number, there was no answer.

'Left some papers in Dr Carling's office,' I offered the porter as I slowly retraced my steps towards the lift and waited outside her consulting room. The door was ajar, and I could hear her talking to someone. I pushed it open. She was not at her desk but leaning against the wall by the window. Perched on one corner of her desk were my diaries, my life's confessions together with her notes in her open briefcase. I heard the call end and I retreated into the hallway.

I retraced my steps, nodded to the porter behind his desk and left.

Outside, I adjusted my hat, as the first spots of rain began to fall with a roll of distant thunder. The sky was darkening quickly as I waited in the shadows of the building opposite. Adrenalin was coursing through my body, accelerating my awareness, and giving me a few moments of strength. I looked up at her office and saw the lights had been extinguished. I waited until I saw her stop under cover of the entrance, putting down her heavy briefcase with my diaries inside, adjusting her yellow umbrella, and the walking into the rain now falling in torrents, drops bouncing off the pavement. I gave her moment's start and followed. I had assumed she would be walking towards the bus station close by, but she veered off into a side street. She was walking quickly, and I had to muster all my waning strength to keep up with her, banging my walking stick as I followed. I began to wonder where she was heading. Thoughts of the police station, handing over my diaries, spiralled through my head. I became anxious and determined to protect myself.

By now my trousers were becoming heavy with water, my walking stick slithered now and again as the rubber end failed to gain a grip on the drenched surfaces. I stumbled once or twice as I tried to keep up. The pavements were crowded with workers scurrying home but still I followed. It was everyone for themselves as we all jostled for space, side-stepping, drifting from the security of the pavement into the gutter streaming with the flow of water. I lost sight of her momentarily as she twisted her umbrella back into shape. She stopped at the edge of the pavement intending to cross. I elbowed my way through the crowd behind her and stood an arms-length away, surveying the road in both directions. The driving conditions were appalling, lights dancing off the glistening tarmac, screen wipers banging to and fro, ineffectual horns blaring. Then came my chance. I grabbed her briefcase that slipped easily from her wet grasp as she turned her face and recognised my smile. I pushed with all my strength hard into the middle of her back. The approaching lorry skidded into the falling body of Dr Barbara Carling, her body bounced off the fender and lay inert as the front wheels bounced over her. I didn't witness the aftermath; I just walked slowly to the bus station and went home.

I sat down exhausted, sipping through a straw a light gin and tonic, relaxing back into my chair. I contented myself in trying to imagine the last moments of her life. Was she walking, thinking of her failure as a mother to understand and spend time with her son? Treat him as she would a patient, like me. Trying to unravel his torment during the early stage of her separation from her husband. I had done my initial research before our first meeting. Her husband had left her when their son was thirteen. I imagined that instead of giving him her support she had gone for furthering her career. Did she regret her negligence and blame herself for her son's death until I came along? She must certainly have been assimilating her options, why else did she have my papers with her? Why else did her death occur within a few hundred metres of the police station on the other side of that fateful road? I believe that as soon as she started to read the details of my excursion to Birmingham, she knew what was coming despite finishing my script. Maybe she never believed her son's death was an accident. There was no trace of the car that caused her son to swerve to his death. She probably did not accept the Coroner's verdict. Now, in those papers she had the means to seek justice for her lost son.

Maybe I am wrong. Perhaps she was already thinking of abandoning her strict code of ethics before we met for the last time and my last revelations tipped her over the edge. There had been times during the last few Sessions that I thought maybe her objective sympathies had altered. There certainly was a hatred in her voice, one I had not encountered before. Now, in those last seconds of her life, she would have encountered excruciating pain, more than flesh and blood can withstand. Her eyes would have fleetingly focussed on her flattened body, once alive and curved, breathing rhythmically, now silent and crushed, then black emptiness. No time for fields of wild flowers, no scent of dew on grass, no heavenly choirs, no time for floating up and back down again to relive the past and return to the future, just everlasting blackness.

EPILOGUE

I was soaked and cold when I arrived home, so I decided to light the log-burner. I poured myself a warm brandy and put the glass to my lips, as I fed the pages of my diaries and contents of my briefcase into the fire, watching the roaring embers of page after page become blackened shads. I picked up the telephone.

'How are things?' I spoke to my children almost every day, but this time it was to be different. I was going to try to be honest.

'Hang on, let me put this on speaker, we're both here. You, okay?'

'Hi, you two. If I said yes, you know I'd be lying.'

'Oh, come on Dad, we know it's not great, but you seemed to have a new lease of life after the scan and transfusion and what did your consultant say? Remind us.'

'Raymond said that I probably gained a few more months if not more.'

'Well, there we are then, another Christmas together, Dad.'

'We all know it is temporary illusion.' I didn't tell them about the latest damning re-scan.

'Anyway, I wanted to tell you something important.'

'What?' they both echoed.

'They found your Mum's murderer. There's closure now.'

'We saw nothing in the paper, what happened?

I could not tell them all the real version of events, so I lied. They had wanted a conclusion as much as I did so I had concocted a believable story.

'You know I'd given up. Every step led to a dead end.'

'You did all you could, Dad.'

'Well, after all the frustration, I visited the same Detective who was in charge of the original investigation. I told him that I had come to the conclusion that the perpetrator was a college student who lived nearby. He agreed that it was a possibility. I also told him of my encounter with the old lady when I was doing my charity leaflet drop and the student, I had met next door.'

'All a bit vague, Dad.'

'Yes, it was until that young man died in a car accident in Birmingham. They discovered at the scene a fluorescent yellow cycling helmet, similar to the one your mother wore. It was too much of a coincidence, so the detective decided to investigate further. The police do not like coincidences. Turns out, he was around at the time, fits the description, drugs were found at his university lodgings together with, would you believe it, your mother's handbag hidden in his wardrobe.'

‘Oh, my God. So that’s it?’

‘Case closed,’ said my daughter.

‘It’s a relief to us all.’

We talked for another half hour or so as I fed the last notes of Dr Carling into the fire, but in the end, I said ‘Sorry, I’m a bit tired, too much excitement for one day. Love you both, remember that, whatever happens.’

‘We love you too.’

I put down the phone and sat back against cushions. I gazed at the log-burner. Nearly all done now, I thought. I looked at the bottle and started to read the accompanying notes. Fentanyl is an opioid and must only be taken under medical supervision. This drug is not only addictive, but it can lead to slowed breathing and death if too much is taken. They should be taken with water and under no circumstances if alcohol is present. When it was prescribed by Raymond Childs to ease my bouts of pain, we had joked about becoming addicted. Now I knew what he meant, I was taking them in greater quantities and more regularly. I remembered his words; “And it doesn't always take extremely excessive use, or even very long-term use, to have a fatal overdose”.

I poured another brandy and went to the bedroom taking the bottle with me. I undressed painfully and got into bed. Put a handful of the pills in my mouth, picked up the glass of brandy and after several attempts managed to swallow them all.

I rested my head against the pillows and adjusted the oxygen mask over my nose and mouth and turned on the flow, my lungs took in the coolness, and I began to relax. Comforted by knowing that my journey through life had been fashioned by circumstances that befallen me over which I seemed to have no control. I closed my eyes as I walked down to the end of the pier, inhaling the salty air, watching the waves break as the wind gusted over the surface then, I heard a loud banging on the door. I tried to move but it was impossible. Then I heard shouting.

'No answer. We know he is here. Execute the warrant, Constable. Get us in there now.'

The front door burst from its hinges as Chief Inspector Woods, Mike Randell and two constables crossed the threshold. Brian Simkins lay to one side, the oxygen mask hissed but little passed into his lungs. His pulse slowed and then there was an eerie silence.

'Too bloody late,' sighed Mike as he turned towards the door where Roger Simmons and Hillary were waiting.

**

Gavin Blackstone QC opened his briefcase and took out one sheet of paper and looked up at Roger Simmons and Mike Randell and the others gathered around the table at MI6 Headquarters.

'I have read all the relevant copy documents that you sent to me including the psychoanalysis evidence. As it happens, not having the originals in the circumstances matters not.

'Here are my conclusions, gentlemen

'Was Brian Simkins predisposed to kill?

'No.

'Did events in his early life make him predisposed to kill?

'Almost certainly.

'Could anything have been done to stop the killings?

'Not in my opinion.

'Could he have been sent to prison for those killings?

'Unlikely.

'Would he be found unfit to plead?

'Undoubtedly.

'What would I recommend now?

'Bury the files, gentlemen.'

**

I am now an impartial but silent observer, and it feels like being wrapped in a warm blanket in a black void. There are no positive feelings, no bad ones either. All your stress, troubles and nightmares have disappeared. Nothing exists in a beautiful welcoming way. If you are reading this now, I am residing in a golden oak plywood box with handles that are already corroding and cracked revealing the plastic that was overlaid with fake gold to make it look good, covered with dark rich soil two metres away from the sweet-smelling grass above that the rain and sun nurtures. My body is already a mess of displaced organs, cuts from neck to pubis sewn with black weaving stitches. My skull sawn into two and my brain minus several parts replaced in the void that was once me. It won't be long before all you see is my six-foot three skeleton, lying bent in the ground surrounded by the last vestiges of a mortal existence. It happens to all of us so do not feel afraid or sorry. Unlike my foetus I can tell you I felt nothing the moment when the permanent darkness descended upon me, and neither will you.

THE END

ACKOWLEDGEMENTS

Thanks to David for guiding me through the pitfalls of computing with his vast knowledge of the science and explaining to me in simple terms how to connect loose ends and to May for her additional incisive input. Any errors are of my own making.

Thanks to Warren Design for juggling my ideas and thoughts into great covers.

To my children, Rachel, Sophie and David, who were never bored with at my constant questioning.

To those at Jericho Writers for their invaluable advice when I started out with Prisoner 441.

But most of all to my wife, Judy, who read the drafts, suggested better ways of expression and wording and kept up my spirits when they were flagging.

My extra special thanks to Diane Bell. I hope I have done her justice with alterations she suggested in this narrative. Thanks, dear friend.

Last but not least to my readers, thank you for your support and to those who have reviewed by books, thanks for taking the trouble, it means a great deal to me.

Printed in Great Britain
by Amazon

71151176R00180